The trial of
PATRICK
SELLAR

The trial of
PATRICK SELLAR

By

IAN GRIMBLE

With an Introduction by
Eric Linklater

SCOTLAND
ALBA

SALTIRE
SOCIETY

First published 1962 by Routledge and Kegan Paul
This paperback edition published 1993 by the Saltire Society,
9 Fountain Close, 22 High Street, Edinburgh EH1 1TF

© Ian Grimble
© The Saltire Society

ISBN 0-85411-053-4

The Publisher acknowledges subsidy from the
Scottish Arts Council towards the publication of this volume.

A catalogue record for this book is available from the British Library

Cover : The portrait of Patrick Sellar is reproduced
by kind permission of the Trustees of the Strathnaver Museum,
Bettyhill. The portrait of the Countess/Duchess of Sutherland by
Thomas Lawrence is in the Sutherland Collection. "The Last
of the Clan" by Thomas Faed is reproduced by permission
of Glasgow Museums : Art Gallery and Museum, Kelvingrove.

Cover design by Smith & Paul Associates, Glasgow

Printed and bound in Great Britain by Cromwell Press Ltd

Contents

————⦿————

Foreword

S I N C E this book was published thirty years ago a large number of studies related to its theme have reached the printed page, culminating in the monumental work of Professor Eric Richards of Flinders University in South Australia. In 1973 he issued his biography of the first Duke of Sutherland, *The Leviathan of Wealth*, in 1982 his first volume of *A History of the Highland Clearances*, followed by the second in 1985. By common consent this is the completest and ablest treatment of the subject ever written.

Richards was able to use the family records catalogued and made available to the public in the Stafford County Record Office. But of the Dunrobin MSS he could inspect only those selected for publication by R. J. Adam, son of the factor to the fifth Duke of Sutherland, who enjoyed exclusive access to this material. It was the present Chief, Elizabeth, Countess of Sutherland, who in 1981 took the step which Richards hailed in his 1985 volume when he wrote 'of the recent deposit of the great Sutherland Collection which will help reconstruct the evidential foundation of modern Highland history.' Richards made what limited use he could of this mass of uncatalogued material, placed at his disposal so late in his studies.

He has done the same with a very different body of evidence, so often ignored or dismissed by Scottish historians. Quoting from *Scottish Gaelic Studies* (1963) he wrote: 'Ian Grimble asserts firmly that "when the history of the Celtic clearances in Scotland is written at last, the voices of Gaels themselves must provide the most important evidence, as they do in the history of all peoples."'' He went on to endorse the verdict of Dr J. L. Campbell, saying: 'The oral tradition, captured in the surviving fragments of Gaelic poetry, expresses something of the collective psyche, and may be claimed to be the richest source relating to the mental world of the peasantry.' He heeded Dr Donald Meek's reminder that 'in the Gaelic Highlands, verse (or more strictly song) rather than prose was until recently the principal medium of popular journalism,' and he gave careful attention to Sorley Maclean's analysis of this material.

Richards selected for approbation Dr James Hunter's *The Making of the Crofting Community* (1976), with its declared aim 'to write the modern history of the Gaelic Highlands from the crofting community's point of view.' Even the distinguished historian Professor A. J. Youngson had contrived in 1973 to publish his major study of the Gaels *After the Forty Five* without consulting a single Gaelic source. In the notes to the following text will be found some of the contemptuous comments of other Lowland academics to this material.

They scoff in particular at the portrait of Patrick Sellar preserved in Gaelic poetry and reflected in these pages. Richards published his verdict in 1985, and it is less easy to dismiss. 'Sellar himself was certainly an objectionable and provocative man; he dislocated the life of the people of Strathnaver in a way which was crude and inhumane. The accommodation for the people he removed from the interior to the coast was not ready until a matter of days before their forced ejection. There is no doubt that Sellar had set fire to at least one house in the strath.' His chapter on the making of the Sellar myth followed the one which I contributed to *History is My Witness*, edited by Gordon Menzies in 1977, and is not at variance with it.

Of those to whom I expressed my gratitude thirty years ago for helping me to understand that verdict, expressed in the language of Sellar's victims, I am happy to say that Robert Mackay, Newlands, remains the President of the Trustees of the Strathnaver Museum. Derick Thomson retired from the Chair of Celtic at Glasgow University in 1991, but remains editor of *Gairm* after more than forty years—surely a record. I renew my heartfelt thanks to both.

Introduction

by ERIC LINKLATER

———————◄••••►———————

THE most incongruous spectacle, and one of the most popular, in contemporary Scotland during the tourist season is the competitive prancing of little girls in a travesty of Gaelic costume on wooden platforms at Highland Gatherings. The dress they wear—kilt and doublet and patterned hose, decorated with frills and laces and small tin medals—is a garish parody of male attire, and the airs to which they dance are the pipe-tunes of a people to whom war was a natural exercise and dancing the social display of a martial spirit. Most of these little girls come from Lowland towns whose inhabitants, until fairly recently, hated, feared, and avoided their Highland neighbours; and finally defeated them. To those who see the history of Scotland as something more than a noisy charade, the appearance of the dancing children is ludicrous and their performance vulgar; but by the majority, not only of foreign visitors but of their fellow Scots, they are often applauded. And in that applause there is a strange discordance.

Even so late as the beginning of the nineteenth century, Scotland was inhabited by two quite different sorts of people. There have been those, within our own time, who have tried to diminish this difference and pretend that all Scotland fetches its strength and spirit from Celtic wombs; while that ingenious and high-tempered dissident, the late Lewis Grassic Gibbon, liked to think we were all Picts. But the gulf between Highlanders and Lowlanders was clearly visible to Walter Scott, and in these pages Ian Grimble quotes that shrewd observer and admirable man, Major-General David Stewart of Garth, who in his *Sketches of the Character, Manners, and Present State of the*

Highlanders of Scotland—published in 1822—wrote with precision: 'For seven centuries Birnam Hill, at the entrance into Athol, has formed the boundary between the Lowlands and the Highlands, and between the Saxon and Gaelic languages. On the south and east sides of the hill, breeches are worn and the Scotch Lowland dialect spoken with as broad an accent as in Mid-Lothian. On the north and west sides are found the Gaelic, the kilt and the plaid, with all the peculiarities of the Highland character.'

But their Gaelic tongue did not unite the Highlanders; nor did their vulnerability to attack by a common enemy. A common danger never inspired in them a thought or policy of self-preservation. The recurrent efforts of the Crown to impose its discipline upon them, and bring them within the scope of a legal and constituted government, never drove them into concerted revolt or persuaded them to cohere in opposition. They never tried to create a separate Highland kingdom, for they were not hostile to the Crown but merely impatient of it. Though they spoke the same language they wore different tartans; and when they required the stimulation of an enemy, they could find one near at hand. As a rule they did no harm to anyone except each other—and from the fourteenth to the seventeenth century life was probably safer in the northern Highlands than in the southern Lowlands—but their narrow loyalties and pastoral habit, their clan chiefs and stubborn preference for freedom, created a large though disparate anachronism, an unresolved and incongruous fraction in the Kingdom of the Scots that was a perpetual irritant and a possible danger to its stability.

From time to time English money or French promises sought allies in the Hebrides, to whose chiefs and chieftains the Lords of the Isles had bequeathed an ineradicable sense of independance; and in the eighteenth century a dynastic cause enlisted in the Highlands enough support to threaten the Hanoverian monarch of the United Kingdom. The Jacobite Rebellion of 1745, defeated at Drummossie Moor in the following year, brought more than retaliation for Charles Edward Stuart's invasion of England; it offered the possibility of retribution for an arrogance which had preferred an effete, unprofitable culture to the disciplines of civilization, and maintained a freedom that insulted more docile neighbours. Nemesis despatched her uncouth lieutenant the Duke of Cumberland to Inverness, and Cumberland with bloody hands inaugurated a policy of planned destruction.

The whole fabric of Highland society was torn to shreds. The clans were disarmed, and forbidden to wear kilt or tartan. The Episcopal clergy were humiliated, and the heritable jurisdictions of the chiefs were abolished. The administration of justice, that is, became the prerogative of the Crown, and the chiefs who had been born to the command of men lived out a diminished life in command of no more than their scanty rents. Not all had been wise or humane in the exercise of their hereditary powers, but abolition of them made the whole clan bankrupt; for what was the worth of a clansman who was under no compulsion to obey? The value of men declined, the value of money went up.

But where was the money to come from? The clan chiefs now had no resources but their land, and their land was encumbered by a host of unprofitable tenants. Temptation came from the south of Scotland, where sheep-farmers had discovered the riches inherent in a flock of Cheviots and wanted more grazing. Cheviots could live and thrive on hill pasture, and the men from the south were willing to pay handsomely for it. But they could not make profitable sheep-runs among hills that were still full of hungry Highlanders. The Highlanders had to go, and go they did. They were, after all, no longer an asset to their chiefs.

The manner in which the clansmen were dispossessed of their holdings varied from place to place. There were chiefs—landowners in fact, but still chiefs in name—who encouraged emigration and allowed a gradual retreat from the overcrowded glens where nothing had ever bred or been domesticated but soldiers and black cattle, the primitive virtues and a great wealth of song. Others, less indulgent and probably stupider, gave a free hand to their factors—most of whom were Lowlanders—and the glens were cleared without mercy. The tacksmen, or tenants-in-chief, were the first to go. They, the gentry of the clan, the near relations of the chief, would not have submitted to the rough demand of an alien factor; and a singular feature of the Clearances is the absence of resistance. In some cases the tacksmen may have been offered compensation or bribed to go; or, being men of education who could translate the writing on the wall, they used what resources they had to seek a kindlier climate. Many found it in North Carolina, and took their sub-tenants with them.

Soon after the battle of Waterloo attention was drawn to the county of Sutherland, where large improvements were being made on the vast estates of the Marquess of Stafford, 'a Leviathan of wealth', and his wife Elizabeth, in her own right Countess of Sutherland. The improvements, it appeared, were being carried out with ruthless efficiency, and the number of people who suffered from them was too large to be ignored. The Sutherland Clearances became notorious, and Ian Grimble has good reasons for re-telling the story of them.

They are more fully documented than similar experiments in other Highland counties; some of which were also extensive and may have been equally devastating. They offer, that is, a detailed picture of some part of a denuding process that changed the physical aspect of the northern counties, as well as forcing upon them a disastrous revolution-from-above. To describe this fragment of the revolution—a revolution which can never be repaired—Ian Grimble has devised a method that in its technique resembles a Chinese nest of boxes; and adopted a tone, not of savage complaint, but of civilized irony.

The trial of Patrick Sellar, sometime the Countess's factor, in Inverness in 1816 was conducted with a bland contempt for justice, and successfully transferred his guilt to the man who had been bold enough to accuse him of malpractice. From this good beginning box after box is extracted, each with some content that enlarges knowledge, and a gallery of surprising characters is released. They range in sort from the monumental hypocrisy (a monument by Chantrey, at the very least) of James Loch, another of the Sutherland factors, to the unexpected, simple anger of an unknown man from Staffordshire; from the honesty and forthright good sense of General Stewart to a glimpse of Sir Walter Scott in a state of nicely controlled ambivalence; from Hugh Miller, the learned stone-mason of Cromarty, to the egregious silliness of Harriet Beecher Stowe, who wrote *Uncle Tom's Cabin* and herself might be a hitherto uncharted character by Dickens; from an old crofter called Angus Mackay, a survivor through tribulation from a golden age, to Evander MacIver, whom Thackeray, if he had extended his observation of snobbery to the Highlands, would have been glad to have invented.

These are some of Ian Grimble's portraits, and the tale that he and they, between them, tell with a sweetly poisoned urbanity is a tale that could have been told with splenetic anger. For it is a tale of tragedy—a tragedy brought about by the blind accumulation of ancient motives, by inhumanity and greed, and sheer stupidity; though from the distance of today stupidity is, of course, seen through the magnifying glass of hind-sight. But the tragedy is indisputable, unrelieved, and irreparable; and because there is no profit in crying over spilt milk, irony is the way to deal with it.

Irony, indeed, is doubly suitable. The nature and character of the victims deserve it, and the consequence of their destruction requires it.

When the United Kingdom of Great Britain and Ireland began to expand into the British Empire, and empire-building, so far from being reprobated,was justly regarded as the growing benignity of a new *pax Romana*, Britain had no better servants than the soldiers of the Highland regiments. From 1745, when the lately mustered Black Watch saved the day at Fontenoy, to the Highland Brigade's dark night at Magersfontein, the regiments who wore a once-prohibited dress fought for their new paymasters with a stern devotion and unfailing valour. 'In the forty years after 1797, *Skye alone* gave the British Army twenty-one lieutenant-generals and major-generals, forty-eight lieutenant-colonels, 600 majors, captains, and subalterns, and 10,000 private soldiers.'* For service of this sort the clans had been trained and tutored, they had learnt their trade as mercenaries in the pay of France and Sweden, of Russia and Prussia and the Netherlands; and when by the Union of the Parliaments in 1707 they were debarred from continental service, they gave, not only the inheritance of their skill at arms, but their unstinted loyalty, to the Crown of Britain.

And what was their reward? By the ignorance, lethargy, and venality of the parliaments of Great Britain their impoverished chiefs or newly rich landlords were allowed to expel them, often in circumstances of great brutality, from the lands which

*Agnes Mure Mackenzie: *Scottish Literature to 1714*.

immemorially were theirs, and whose traditions had nurtured their valour. And how should an honest historian deal with such a monstrous betrayal except by a roar of unavailing anger, or judgment on the quiet scale of irony?   .

Mark also the consequence of their expulsion. In 1782 the decrees prohibiting tartan and the wearing of the kilt were rescinded, and in 1822 when George IV came to Edinburgh, to a festival stage-managed by Sir Walter, the old Highland dress became suddenly fashionable, and tailors ever since have been busily inventing new tartans. Proud Lowland lords who, in 1700, would rather have seen their children dead than arrayed in Celtic finery, have wrapped alien kilts about their waists, and registered the sett under Saxon or Norman names. Queen Victoria, unashamedly romantic—riding plump and gallant on her Highland journeys—had all Balmoral swathed in a tartan designed by her gravely brilliant Consort. And in the course of time, as the old Highland Gatherings became popular, money-making affairs, a rout of little girls appeared to prance on resounding wooden platforms, in a travesty of Highland dress, and be applauded by Lowland neighbours whose ancestors may have run helter-skelter from a Highland charge.

The Highlanders were defeated, the Highland way of life was destroyed; but the proscribed tartans survived to become the recognized vesture of Scotland. What also has survived, into this century, is something of the grace and gallantry and gaiety that distinguished the arrogant, stark-poor, singing clans; and proof of that survival is in the history of the Highland Division in two wars, or can be heard at any village *ceilidh*, or read in the pages of this book. For Ian Grimble has given his tragedy the grace-notes of irony and wit, and they enhance it with the propriety of the grace-notes in that great pibroch, *The Lament for the Children*.

Anns an adhar dhubh-ghorm ud,
Airde na sìorraidheachd os ar cionn,
Bha rionnag a' priobadh ruinn,
'S i freagairt mireadh an teine
Ann an cabair tigh m' athar
A' bhliadhna thugh sinn an tigh le bleideagan sneachda.

Agus sud a' bhliadhna cuideachd
A shlaod iad a' chailleach do'n t-sitig,
A shealltainn cho eòlach 's a bha iad air an Fhìrinn,
Oir bha nid aig eunlaith an adhair
(Agus cròthan aig na caoraich)
Ged nach robh àit aice-se anns an cuireadh i a ceann fòidhpe.

A Shrath Nabhair 's a Shrath Chill Donnain
Is beag an t-iongnadh ged a chinneadh am fraoch àluinn oirbh,
A' falach nan lotan a dh' fhàg Pàdraig Sellar 's a sheòrsa,
Mar a chunnaic mi uair is uair boireannach cràbhaidh
A dh' fhiosraich dòrainn an t-saoghail-sa
Is sìth Dhé 'na sùilean.

RUARAIDH MAC THOMAIS
1960

1

What the Judge Said
1816

———◆◆◆◆———

T HE Court had sat since ten o'clock in the morning on Tuesday, the 23rd April 1816, and by the time the jury returned their verdict it was after midnight. But the court-room at Inverness was still densely crowded as the Lord Commissioner of Justiciary, Lord Pitmilly, addressed the prisoner at the bar.

'Mr. Sellar, it is now my duty to dismiss you from the bar; and you have the satisfaction of thinking that you are discharged by the unanimous opinion of the Jury and the Court. I am sure that, although your feelings must have been agitated, you cannot regret that this trial took place; and I am hopeful it will have due effect on the minds of the country, which have been so much and so improperly agitated.'

The crimes of which Patrick Sellar had been acquitted were culpable homicide, real injury, and oppression. The jury had taken a quarter of an hour to reach their unanimous verdict. Eight of them were local landed proprietors, two of them merchants, two tacksmen, and one of them a lawyer.

The proceedings had been tediously prolonged by the numbers of witnesses who only understood the native language of the country. Their evidence had had to be translated into English by a Sheriff-Substitute before it could be understood either by the judge or by many, if not all, of the jurors. But as Lord Pitmilly emphasized, their labour had been well spent. Horrible calumnies had been circulated about the factor of one

1

of Scotland's largest estates. They could not but reflect on his noble employers, and these were no less than the Marquess of Stafford and his wife Elizabeth, in her own right Countess of Sutherland.

It was the year after Waterloo, and men whose Highland dress had spread fear and admiration throughout Europe were returning to the peace of their native glens. 'My brave Highlanders, remember your country, remember your forefathers,' Sir John Moore had once called to them in the heat of battle. They were returning now to the land of their forefathers since time immemorial.

Few had a longer journey from their depots than the inhabitants of Strathnaver, the northernmost region on the Scottish mainland. The majority of these were Mackays, though Macleods were also numerous in the west, Gunns in the east, and Gordons along the southern marches. East of Strathnaver lay the less mountainous county of Caithness, and south of these the rather smaller county of Sutherland.

Here stood the great castle of Dunrobin, the principal Scottish seat of the Countess of Sutherland.

Her surname was Gordon and her forebears had acquired the Sutherland earldom in the sixteenth century. To it they had added much church property at the reformation. Later they had obtained the overlordship of the Mackay country of Strathnaver also.[1] But it was more recently that they had begun to purchase the freehold of large tracts of the Mackay country. It was the fortune of the Marquess of Stafford that opened the prospect of one huge Sutherland embracing Strathnaver also, entirely owned by the lords of Dunrobin.

Strathnaver was a Celtic country, and few of its inhabitants understood any language except Gaelic. The Gordon Earls of Sutherland were of Lowland origin, and it appears that none of them learned the language of a people over whom they had for long exercised a capital jurisdiction. On the contrary, they considered it their duty to root out the Gaelic barbarity on their estates, and substitute the English civility of which they were among the most northern exponents. So a Gordon had written at Dunrobin as early as 1630. The present Countess Elizabeth had shown her respect for his attitude by issuing a sumptuous volume of his writings in 1813.

Neither did she neglect his injunctions, nor fail to interest her English husband in them. The agent they chose to transform their northern estates was William Young, from the lands they could see across the water from Dunrobin. Young was an astute self-made man who had improved the valueless property of Inverugie in Morayshire. His proposal for the development of the Stafford estates in Strathnaver was that they should be cleared entirely of their inhabitants, except on coastal strips, and given over to sheep instead. He was appointed commissioner of the estate to supervise this improvement, and Patrick Sellar joined him from Morayshire to act as legal agent and accountant. The partnership began in 1810 and prospered to the extent that Patrick Sellar was himself able to bid in 1813 for the huge sheep farm carved out of the populous district between Loch Naver and Badenloch.

The natives, however, proved ungrateful. There were riots, or rumours of them, and troops were sent to defend Dunrobin. Disrespectful allegations about the running of Lady Sutherland's estate appeared in newpapers, and several people in Strathnaver raised a subscription to meet the expense of prosecuting Sellar.

Some of the tenants on Patrick Sellar's new sheep farm petitioned the Countess herself, who 'was graciously pleased to return an answer in writing' on the 22nd July 1814. She declared 'that if any person on the estate shall receive any illegal treatment, she will never consider it as hostile to her if they have recourse to legal redress'. She added that she had forwarded the complaint to Mr. Sellar, desiring that he should report to her after making inquiries. There was an obvious flaw in this solution, which the disaffected tried to remedy by sending a second petition to Lord Gower, the son of the Countess. On the 8th February 1815 Lord Gower replied that he had shown the petition to his parents, who had forwarded it this time to their other factor, William Young.

But they took a more fateful step to expose the malicious rumours that were appearing in the Press, and to silence the agitators who sought to wreck the scheme of improvement. They ordered Young to place the matter in the hands of the Sheriff-Depute of Sutherland. A pronouncement on the legality of these proceedings would be conclusive.

It happened that the Sheriff-Depute was absent from Sutherland during most of the spring of 1815. The Sheriff-Substitute was a man named Robert Mackid, a Gael able to converse with the aboriginal inhabitants who were being removed. To this initial source of prejudice, the jurors learned, he added want of judgement: he hurried into Strathnaver and took evidence from about forty aggrieved tenants. But as Sellar's counsel at the trial pointed out, Mackid suffered from an even graver defect of character: he was actuated by personal malice against Sellar. The jurors could confirm this for themselves when the letter that Mackid wrote to the Marquess of Stafford on the 30th May 1815 was read out in court. 'I have to inform your Lordship, that a more numerous catalogue of crimes, perpetrated by an individual, has seldom disgraced any country . . . the laws of the country imperiously call upon me to order Mr. Sellar to be arrested and incarcerated, in order for trial, and before this reaches your Lordship, this preparatory legal step must be put in execution.' The respectable jury of landowners and merchants listened to this description of one of their social order, and to the treatment he had received, so reminiscent of the worst excesses of Jacobinism. They heard the list of crimes of which Mackid had accused him.

'1. Wilful fire-raising; by having set on fire and reduced to ashes a poor man's whole premises, including dwelling-house, barn, kiln, and sheep cot, attended with most aggravated circumstances of cruelty, if not murder.

'2. Throwing down and demolishing a mill, also a capital crime.

'3. Setting fire to and burning the tenants' heath pasture, before the legal term of removal.

'4. Throwing down and demolishing houses, whereby the lives of sundry aged and bed-ridden persons were endangered, if not actually lost.

'5. Throwing down and demolishing barns, kilns, sheep cots etc. to the great hurt and prejudice of the owners.

'6. Innumerable other charges of lesser importance swell the list.'

The first charge alone contained the capital crimes of arson and possibly of murder, and in the crowded court-room at Inverness it remained to be seen what sort of people would come forward with evidence of such enormities against a factor of Lord and Lady Stafford. The first witness to be called was William Chisholm, for whom the Sheriff-Substitute of Ross-shire was sworn as interpreter, since Chisholm spoke no English. The witness described how Sellar had come to his home in June 1814, nearly two years before, with twenty men besides four sheriff-officers, who had pulled down and set fire to the house and its barns. His mother-in-law, Margaret Mackay, was still in the house when it was set on fire, for she was a hundred years old and bed-ridden, although she was not ill. It was Sellar himself who ordered the house to be fired. 'Sellar', so the interpreter summarized Chisholm's account, 'desired the woman to be taken out, although she should not live one hour after. It was in about two minutes after this that witness's sister-in-law came and took out the old woman. The blankets in which she was wrapped were burnt, and the bed was going on fire before she was taken out. She said, "God receive my soul: what fire is this about me?" and never spoke a word more.'

Chisholm's wife, Henrietta Mackay, was also called as a witness. She had been away from home when the factor's party arrived, and returned in terror when she saw the smoke rising from the distance. But one of her children had run to meet her and told her that her mother was safe. She gave her mother's age as ninety-two. They had placed her in a small byre that had no door and a thatched roof which was partly 'spoiled', and here Margaret Mackay died five days later without ever uttering another word. John Mackay, a third witness, deposed that he had told Sellar there was an old woman in the house who could not be removed. 'Sellar said that she must be taken away.' He also confirmed that the last words she ever spoke were uttered as she was being carried out of the burning house, though he gave them as 'O teine' (Oh fire).

Chisholm stated in evidence that Sellar had given him three shillings, while another of the party 'also gave him other three shillings from Mr. Sellar, as he said, for the timber'. At this point the published report of the trial supplements Chisholm's evidence with information he is not likely to have given in this form himself to the Court. 'By the practice of the country,' the reader is told as though Chisholm were himself expounding Scots law, 'the outgoing tenant is entitled to carry away the timber belonging to the house, unless the incoming tenant pays for it.' But Chisholm stated that he had accepted this payment after his timber had already been burned. Both he and his wife also deposed that they possessed three pound notes, either in a chest or in a hole in the wall, which were lost.

It is impossible to recapture the impression these three witnesses made in the court-house of Inverness. The majesty of the law must have been the more intimidating to them because its complicated formalities were conducted in a foreign language. They differed over the age of the old woman, gave a time of day and then admitted they did not possess a watch, varied suspiciously in their accounts of where the three lost pounds had been secreted. Nor could their appearance have recommended them. They had always been poor and for nearly two years they had been destitute.

Patrick Sellar by contrast produced in court overwhelming evidence of his reputability, A letter was read from Brodie of Brodie describing Sellar as 'a person of the strictest integrity and humanity, incapable of being even accessory to any cruel or oppressive action'.[2] Sir George Abercromby of Birkenbog, Baronet, wrote that he had known Sellar since childhood. 'I have always thought him a young man of great humanity, and I think him incapable of being guilty of the charges brought against him, and trust, upon trial, they will turn out to be unfounded, and put a stop to that clamour which was so disagreeable.' The Sheriff-Substitute of Elgin and Nairn had also known Sellar from a boy, 'and I have always known him to be a man of sympathy, feeling, and humanity'.

These were judgements to move the most impartial jury, and they were reinforced by the Sheriff-Substitute of Inverness in person, who deposed that 'he has known the pannel from his boyhood. He has borne a most respectable character, and is known to witness to be of a humane disposition. Witness conceives him incapable of doing anything cruel or oppressive.' Sir Archibald Dunbar of Northfield, Baronet, then entered the witness-box to say the same.

It was scarcely necessary. The undoubted legality of most of Sellar's actions in this case was easily established without reference to his personal character. William Young had already embarked on the scheme of improvement for the south end of the

Naver valley before Sellar himself applied for tenancy of the huge sheep farm it was proposed to establish there. William Young had given public notice of this at Golspie in Sutherland as early as December 1813. Because much of this well-populated area lay in the Strathnaver parish of Farr, the Rev. David Mackenzie, minister of the parish, had been instructed to explain the notice in Gaelic to the inhabitants. Respect for the minister of God was profound amongst his pious flock, and if they found the ordinance of eviction hard to bear, he was able to comfort them with the message that all things are ordained of God and that hardship is a divine visitation for man's sins.

But whether or not the people of the upper Naver were in a state of grace to co-operate in the scheme of improvement, they had no alternative in law but to do so. The absolute title to the lands their race had probably occupied since before the days of the Vikings was the property of the Countess of Sutherland and Marchioness of Stafford. They were merely her tenants, and when she handed the tenancy of the lands of Kildonan and Farr in which they lived to her factor Patrick Sellar, they ceased to be tenants. She owed them no further responsibility, and if she nevertheless offered to settle them elsewhere on her estates, this was a mere act of generosity.

Evidence was given in court that such indeed were the generous intentions of the Countess-Marchioness, and that her factors had already laboured to carry them out. The notice of removal published in December 1813, and translated by the minister of Farr to his parishioners, stated exactly where the evicted might settle. 'Lord and Lady Stafford have directed that all the grounds from Curnachy on the north and Dunviden on the south side of the river down to its mouth, including Swordly and Kirtomy, with a sufficient quantity of pasture, is to be lotted out among them, and in which every person of good character will be accommodated.' (Kirtomy was spelt Kirktomy in this notice, an interesting example of the improving attitude of these lowland factors to the Strathnaver place-names. There was never a church—or kirk in the lowland dialect of English—at Kirtomy, and had there been, it would have possessed a name containing the Gaelic *Cill* for church; as at Balnakil along the coast to the west.)

In these lands extending to the mouth of the Naver river,

and along the north coast of Strathnaver to the east of it, persons of good character were privileged to build new homes. By a further gesture of philanthropy they were even permitted to take from their former homes, without payment, building materials that were the property of the Countess-Marchioness at the termination of a tenancy. For it was only the posts or joists of time-hardened bog-fir, dug from the peat moors, that the inhabitants themselves owned. All the timber taken from growing trees belonged to the Countess, like the woods from which they derived. But she had graciously signified that they might carry this away with them to the sites of their new homes.

It was in this context that the Rev. David Mackenzie, whose manse stood at Bettyhill in the centre of the area of new allotments, gave some disquieting evidence to the Court. The notice had promised all who had notice to quit that their allotments would be ready by Whitsunday. It was none too soon, for as Sellar himself testified, he was extremely anxious to take possession that spring. 'In the beginning of the month of May the declarant (Sellar) extracted the decreets, and caused charge the defenders in terms of the decreets; . . . he thereafter obtained precepts of ejection, and after waiting till about three weeks after the term, he was under the unpleasant necessity of putting the warrants into the hands of the officers of Court, and employing them to make the premises void and redd.' The minister of Farr recalled in the witness-stand that Sellar had remarked to him at that time: 'they were dilatory in removing, to which the witness rejoined that the allotments were not ready on the very day of Whitsunday, and this prevented them from moving'.

William Young entered the witness-stand immediately after the minister had mentioned this unfortunate mishap, and explained why there had been a delay in laying out the allotments by the promised date. A surveyor had been sent to examine the ground in April, but his wife's illness had taken him from his work, and it was not until the end of May that Young himself had been free to visit Strathnaver. 'By the 4th of June', Young was able to reasssure the jurors, 'everything was ready for the reception of the people.' No one asked for details of what he implied by 'everything', nor did the Court pause to relate Sellar's haste at one end of the strath with the surveyor's

8

delay at the other. The minister's remark was treated as though it had been an indiscretion not to be pursued without disrespect.

Or perhaps the Court recognized that fundamentally it was irrelevant, inasmuch as the allotments, as the notice of removal explained, were distributed to persons of good character only. 'Chisholm the tinker got none,' William Young related, 'because for two years back complaints had been made against him as a worthless character.' It was not necessary for Young to tell the Court who had brought such complaints, what they contained, whether the term tinker was intended to convey a specific meaning, or whether it was simply pejorative. The Countess-Marchioness was not obliged to accommodate him and his dependants on her estates whatever his character, and she or her servants could assess it as loosely as they cared. Patrick Sellar was more specific, as was only natural, because according to Chisholm's evidence he had committed arson and murder. Sellar deposed that Chisholm 'had married, and lived in family with a second wife in the lifetime of the first, who had lately visited him in company with some other tinkers'. Many domestic habits that appear intriguing in the rich and fashionable have a more reprehensible appearance when adopted by the poor, and in the Regency period during which this trial took place Sellar's second-hand gossip at Chisholm's expense no doubt had its effect. Sellar added that Chisholm 'was a reputed thief' and was not challenged to prove either allegation.

All that concerned the Court was whether at Chisholm's home in the June of 1814 Sellar had committed arson of a dwelling-house to the danger of an old woman's life. Of all the rumours in the country, all the accusations in the Press, all the charges of Robert Mackid, this was the only one that had penetrated to the court-room at Inverness in a form that presented any real danger to Patrick Sellar. It rested on the evidence of a tinker, a worthless character, a reputed thief: it was supported by Henrietta Mackay, his wife—if she was his wife. The only other witness was one John Mackay.

Against their testimony the defence called several past and present estate employees, indicating 'that a vast number of additional witnesses in exculpation were in attendance'. One remembered that the old woman had cried out as she was carried from the house, and that there was already smoke issuing from it. 'But this seemed to arise from the divots falling from the roof on the fire.' He meant by this that the house was partly dismantled while a fire still burned in the hearth. Sellar, all agreed, had reached the house after the woman had been removed from it, but before it had been destroyed. Sellar had insisted on the house's destruction, a witness recalled, because Chisholm would otherwise have rebuilt it. For that reason Sellar had paid Chisholm the value of the bog-fir and had burnt it with all the other wood torn from the building. The witnesses emphasized that there had been 'no unnecessary cruelty'. There had been some conversation as to what would become of the old woman, but no mention was made of the children who were presumably rendered homeless also. No witness denied that a woman of ninety-two had died after five days in the little horse-byre with no door and a leaking roof. That in itself was no concern of Sellar's.

Lord Pitmilly in his summing-up directed the jury to ignore all of the charges except two. One concerned the destruction of barns, and in this case Sellar had ignored a custom of the country, but had not infringed the law of Scotland. The other concerned the house of Chisholm, and here his Lordship reminded the jury that 'this witness, although contradicted in some particulars by his wife, was confirmed by John Mackay'. The jury must decide between their evidence and that of the defence witnesses. 'His Lordship also said that if the jury were at all at a loss on this part of the case, they ought to take into view the character of the accused; for this was always of importance in balancing contradictory testimony. Now here there was, in the first place, real evidence, from the conduct of Mr. Sellar, in regard to the sick, for this in several instances had been proved to be most humane. And secondly, there were the letters of Sir George Abercromby, Mr. Brodie, and Mr. Fenton, which although not evidence'— this remark of Lord Pitmilly's is most noteworthy—'must have some weight with the jury: and there were the testimonies of Mr. Gilzean and Sir Archibald Dunbar—all establishing Mr. Sellar's humanity of disposition.' Having added his own testimony in such unmistakable terms, Lord Pitmilly waited a quarter of an hour for the verdict.

When it was given 'Lord Pitmilly observed that his opinion completely concurred with that of the jury'. He returned to

Edinburgh supposing, probably, that he had said the final word and silenced that clamour which was so disagreeable.

Sellar took even more effective measures to complete his vindication. He brought a suit for libel against Robert Mackid in Edinburgh, who had already been compelled to resign the office of Sheriff-Substitute of Sutherland, and who had retired with his destitute family to Thurso. Mackid was forced to settle with Sellar on his own terms in order to escape deeper ruin. He agreed to pay the expenses of Sellar's suit and £200 in addition: he also wrote Sellar a letter of apology that was deposited in the sheriff court of Dornoch as a probative writ, so that all posterity might read there of the innocence of Patrick Sellar.

'Being impressed with the perfect conviction and belief that the statements to your prejudice, contained in the precognition which I took in Strathnaver in May 1815 were to such an extent exaggerations as to amount to absolute falsehoods, I am free to admit that, led away by the clamour excited against you, on account of the discharge of the duties of your office, as factor for the Marchioness of Stafford, in introducing a new system of management on the Sutherland estate, I gave a degree of credit to those misstatements of which I am now thoroughly ashamed, and which I most sincerely and deeply regret. . . .'

Patrick Sellar probably supposed that this was the end of the matter. In fact, it was hardly the beginning.

2

What the Factor Said

1820

━━━◆◆◆◆━━━

STRATHNAVER, the country in which Patrick Sellar was now free to make his fortune, is rightly considered to be one of the most beautiful, and disturbing, in the British Isles. Its name has vanished from the modern maps, but the curious will find that in maps of the seventeenth and eighteenth centuries the region comprised the greater part of the present county of Sutherland. And where the plains of Caithness crumble beyond Dounreay into little foothills and a road sign announces the Sutherland border, the traveller is really entering Strathnaver. A cleft rock by the roadside tells him this, if he is able to read a landmark without inscription. The rock marks the ancient boundary between the Celtic Highlands of Strathnaver and the Norse lands of Caithness and the islands.

Along the north coast of Scotland the foothills crease in ever-deepening valleys until they reach the largest and most fertile of them all, with the Naver river running through it. To the west again Ben Loyal rears its great granite buttresses above the Kyle of Tongue. The undulations steepen: the coastal indentations become deeper. Ben Hope's half-moon summit leans towards Loch Eriboll, and beyond this long sea-loch the mountains form an unbroken chain from Cape Wrath down the west coat to the Assynt border. From here the Celtic Hebrides are visible beyond the Minch, just as the Norse Orkneys are visible across the Pentland Firth from further east.

Throughout this land the crofter cutting peats or taking his sheep to the moor, the lobster fisherman dropping his creels, the tenant of the new council house who travels the coast road to work at Dounreay, all have a view of almost their entire land in every direction. Strathnaver is larger than many British counties, yet it is spread out before them like a map, the great rock bastions beyond Loch Eriboll, Ben Klibreck on the southern marches, the headlands of the Moine and Strathy Point with innumerable promontories thrusting their prows into the turbulent seas between.

The gigantic panorama is ever-changing. There are the still days of summer when the *primula-scotica*, a minute primrose, blossoms on the only headland in the world where it will grow. Wild scabious turns the sandy coastal fields to mauve before the haymaking and the sea becomes a still, Mediterranean blue. There are the wild days of the spring equinox when winds trample the young growth before the lambing, changing speed and direction with furious suddenness. The spray then cascades hundreds of feet over the headlands, and separate storms can be seen wheeling and sparring among the mountains and far out to sea. Between storms the air has a clarity that sharpens every outline to a knife-edge in the brief interval of sunshine.

Strathnaver may still turn white at this time, but the snow will rarely lie long. It is during the weeks after the New Year that the snow-plough teams expect their hardest work to begin. From the winter snowstorms the country emerges a desert of dazzling white between orange sky and pewter sea, and its most distant contours often remain visible at night beneath the moon. But the most tremendous of spectacles will appear with the northern lights along the horizon: when the *Fir Clis*, the merry dancers, move in ever-changing procession like the medieval chain-dancers to a heroic ballad. The crofter's wife will pause in the cold night air on her way to peat-stack or to byre, although she has seen this sight many times before.

The coast road passes through villages beyond time that enchant the traveller. Few of them run inland down the empty straths, but wherever they run may be seen the crumbling stone-work, the fields once drained and dug over which the bracken is so fast encroaching, and sometimes a park that shines green in the distance as though it were tended still.

Patrick Sellar entered this country from the south. At

Whitsunday in 1810 he obtained a lease of the farm of Morvich on the east coast of Sutherland, a few miles from Dunrobin Castle. At Whitsunday in 1814 he took possession of the extensive lands of the Abrach Mackays east of the Naver river, where William Chisholm lived. After his acquittal, at Whitsunday in 1819, he occupied the whole of the west side of the Naver river for a distance of some twenty miles from Loch Naver to the sea. Only the small township of Invernaver at the river-mouth was exempted, because of its usefulness as a salmon-fishing station. He had resigned his factorship in the previous year in order to devote himself to the exploitation of his huge properties, and in future he served the Staffords only as an independent contractor.

In 1820 he wrote an account of his extraordinary success. It had its origins only eleven years earlier when Sellar, a young man in his late twenties belonging to the English-speaking area of north-east Scotland, had visited Celtic Scotland for the first time in his life. 'In May 1809 Mr. Young and I and several other Morayshire men embarked, to see this *terra incognita.* We came into Dunrobin Bay in a beautiful morning, a little after sunrise; and I shall never forget the effect produced upon us by the beauty of the scenery—the mountains, rocks, wood, and the castle reflected on the sea as from a mirror.'

They stayed about a week, surveying the east coast of Sutherland, and while its scenery pleased them, its people did not. 'The Gaelic seemed universally the language of the country; which reposed under the domination of the old half-pay officers and other tacksmen, who held it by their sub-tenants.' The whole structure of society was utterly archaic. 'The people seemed to be all of one profession, that is to say, every man was his own mason, carpenter, tanner, shoemaker. . . . Every man wore his own cloth, ate his own corn and potatoes, sold a lean kyloe to pay the rent; had no ambition for any comfort or luxury beyond the sloth he then possessed.' Sellar heard of the experiment in sheep farming that had been started that spring between Lairg and Ben Klibreck by two men from Northumberland. 'We heard mentioned with execration the names of some Englishmen for whom, in the interior of the country, many families had been removed nearer to the coast to give place to sheep farming; but it seemed the general belief that their stay in the country would be short.' In the following spring Patrick Sellar began the career in this country which ended only with his death.

He diagnosed instantly the best interests of the people among whom he came to live, and found them to correspond exactly with his own. 'I was at once a convert to the principle now almost universally acted on in the highlands of Scotland, viz. that the people should be employed in securing the natural riches of the sea-coast; that the mildew of the interior should be allowed to fall upon grass, and not upon corn; and that several hundred miles of Alpine plants, flourishing in these districts, in curious succession at all seasons, and out of the *reach of anything but sheep*, be converted into wool and mutton for the English manufacturer.' He did not mention the alternative, that the natural inhabitants might keep sheep while he went fishing.

But perhaps he intended to suggest that he had left them the richer prize of the two. 'Let any person, I don't care who he be, or what his prejudices, let him view the inside of one of the new fishermen's stone cots in Loth—the man and his wife and young children weaving their nets around their winter fire. Let him contrast it with the sloth, and poverty, and filth, and sleep of an unremoved tenant's turf hut in the interior. Let him inspect the people, stock, cattle, horses, trees and plants in a stock farmer's possession, and compare it with the pared bottom from which turf in all ages had been taken, with the closely cropped roots of grass, and bushes and miserable lazy-bed's culture that surround a highlander's cabin . . . and let him *believe*, if he can, that men are injured by civilization, and that during the last ten years a most important benefit has not been conferred on this country.'

If Sellar wrote with sincerity, he did not stoop to a pettifogging accuracy in his arguments. Thus, a fisherman in Loth was hardly comparable with an unremoved tenant in Strathnaver, because these were not drafted to Loth on the east coast of Sutherland. They were given allotments on the north coast, where there were no natural or artificial harbours, and where many of them had to carry earth on their backs to construct minute patches of cultivable land among the rocks. These were men of good character, however this might be assessed: men like William Chisholm had nowhere to go.

But it is the second part of Sellar's comparison that really reveals the nature of his mission. Let anyone inspect the people of the new stock farms, he says, and compare them with the Gaels they have supplanted. The benefit he had conferred on the country was not that he had denuded it of inhabitants, but that he had cleared it of aboriginals, so that it could be enjoyed and exploited by English-speaking lowlanders. 'In place of the few scores (perhaps from two to three score) of highland families who have since emigrated, I am convinced there are five scores of south country families imported; and that a trial will show no diminution of people in 1820.'

But it was not Sellar who in 1820 published the grand apologia of the Sutherland improvements. The letter in which he outlined some of his principles and methods was merely an appendix to this impressive volume, the work of James Loch.

James Loch was born in the same year as Patrick Sellar, but while Sellar was reared in Morayshire and studied law in Edinburgh, Loch was born in Edinburgh and studied English law in London. It took him a little longer to secure his entry into the mammoth organization of the Stafford-Sutherland estates at its southern end. He became an auditor in 1811, the year after Sellar had established himself in the farm of Morvich. William Young resigned from his factorship in the year of Sellar's trial, to resume his private enterprises, and when Patrick Sellar took the same course the position of exponent and executive of the Sutherland improvements lay open to James Loch.

Loch entitled his publication *An account of the improvements on the estates of the Marquess of Stafford in the counties of Stafford and Salop, and on the estate of Sutherland.* This second part is the principal one, and in it Loch described the first experiment of 1807, the larger clearances up to the time of Sellar's trial, the recent removals that had completed the grand design.

The intention of his book was explained by its title: to describe the economic revolution carried out on the estates of Lord and Lady Stafford, and the benefits bestowed on the country and its people. But a second and very different purpose asserts itself so obtrusively as to turn every other page into a battle-ground. Even the inscription, before the book is yet begun, reveals these rival objectives in fierce embrace. 'It was incumbent on me to give some account of the nature and progress of those measures (now that they are completed), which Your Lordship and Lady Stafford had adopted for the improvement of the estate of Sutherland, in order to contradict, in the most positive and direct manner, the unfounded and unwarrantable statements; or, perhaps, I shall be more correct if I were to say, the artful perversions of the truth which have been circulated in regard to this subject.' Thereafter Loch did not allow the reader to forget for more than a few pages at a time that the great philanthropists he served were martyrs to ingratitude and malice. If his gospel is authentic, then Dunrobin was the occasional retreat of saints much tried by devils.

No summary of James Loch's thesis would do justice to its author if it suppressed the devils, for this would give the impression that the Staffords and their factors had won a respite from whispering liars and mischievous agitators since the vindication of Sellar in 1816. Loch's statement of the truth was intended to achieve what the trial had failed to do. 'In giving the following account', he reached the point of saying by page 12, 'of the humane and considerate views which have regulated the management of this great and rapidly improving property, no further notice will be taken of these mis-statements, except in so far as may be necessary to show what they are here stated distinctly to be, *totally and completely false.*' Italics, capitals, and even long footnotes were invoked to frighten the devils away.

The benefits with which Loch opened his account needed no special eloquence to recommend them. There was the bridge built by Telford at Bonar to carry the new road from Inverness into Sutherland. It was completed in 1812, and the road over the Ord into Caithness was finished in 1814, and another to Tongue on the north coast of Strathnaver by 1820. With roads came mails, and the first mail-coach ran between Inverness and Thurso in July 1819. The coaches required resting-places for horses and travellers; Loch's account is illustrated by the architects' plans of the inns built along the forty-mile stretch of the route that passed through eastern Sutherland. Where the road reached the obstacle of Loch Fleet a gigantic causeway was constructed across the shallow water.

Some of these schemes were promoted by the heritors of other counties, as Loch explained, and most of them were subsidized by the Government. But Stafford, an Englishman, had been tireless in supporting them, and he contributed largely from his English fortune towards the cost of their completion.

It remained to modernize the land and its people, and to the factor from Edinburgh one of the largest obstacles to this was the native language: 'that barrier which the prevalence of the Celtic tongue presents to the improvement and civilization of the district, wherever it may prevail'. It was, he said, 'a language in which no book was ever written'. To recall the first publication of a Gaelic prose work in Scotland in 1567; the three contemporary editions of the poetry of Duncan Macintyre whom Loch might have seen in Edinburgh; to recall Rob Donn Mackay in his tomb in Strathnaver, while the manuscript of his poetry awaited publication in its first edition of 1829, to harp upon such facts would be to nurse irrelevancies. James Loch stated very clearly what was relevant to him. The landlords of an exclusively Gaelic Highland estate were determined to banish the Celtic darkness with the bright beams of English light.

The cause was nothing less than advancing civilization and its nexus in the north was not the indigenous Celtic society of the Highlanders, but the immensely powerful organization based at Dunrobin. Until very recently the Highlanders had indeed been able to contribute usefully to this family organization. 'The Earls of SUTHERLAND continued to find, that the principal means by which they had to maintain that station in the country which their rank and descent entitled them to hold, was, by raising for the service of government, one of those corps, well known by the designation of a "family regiment".' But the house of Sutherland had found other ways to maintain its station. 'As the country advanced in civilization, other objects of ambition arose, which money alone could procure. And the population of the highlands remained no longer an object to be encouraged beyond that point, which was required for the necessary demands for labour on the estate, or to realize a money rent.'

Unfortunately the population, particularly in the Mackay country of Strathnaver, was greatly in excess of Dunrobin's present requirements. It was augmented by those who had returned from the Napoleonic war with such distinction, and it possessed a social structure that was not conducive to realizing a money rent by the best approved methods of the day.

Sub-infeudation was the greatest evil to which James Loch drew attention, and the position of the tacksman, or lease-holders, in this antique pattern of society he condemned utterly. 'That portion of their rent which was payable in kind, or in money, (the former being by far the most common,) was obtained by their sub-letting part of their lands, in the most exorbitant manner. They extracted from their subtenants services which were of the most oppressive nature, and to such an extent, that if they managed well, they might hold what they retained in their own occupation, rent-free. This saved them from a life of labour and exertion. The whole economy of their farm, securing their fuel, gathering their harvest, and grinding their corn, were performed by their immediate dependants.' As the improvement of the Sutherland estates depended upon the removal of these oppressive middlemen, it was not surprising that the most determined opposition had arisen from such a quarter. 'This expectation has not been disappointed; and it is from individuals of this class, and persons connected with them, that those false and malignant representations have proceeded, which have been so loudly and extensively circulated. Actuated by motives of a mere personal nature, regardless of the happiness of the people, whose improvement it was the great object of the landlord to effect, they attempted to make an appeal in favour of a set of people who were never before the objects of their commiseration, in order that they might, if possible, reduce them, for their own selfish purposes, to that state of degradation from which they had been just emancipated.' The views of the Gaelic gentry and intelligentsia could be discounted, though not all of them. Some had 'embraced with alacrity the new scene of active exertion presented for their adoption; seconding the views of the landlords with the utmost zeal, marked with much foresight and prudence'.

Among the returning soldiers the forces of good and evil contended likewise. 'Many of the discharged men of the 93d entertained the expectation, although well and liberally re-warded by the bounty of the nation, that they should still have obtained farms in the same manner as those who, after having served the views and forwarded the interests of their Chief, had tacks of land granted to them.' These men had learned English on their service abroad, which Loch now found to be a blessing not without its attendant dangers. 'Possessed of the rudiments of education, by being able to read and write, and above all having acquired the advantage of the use of the English language, they became advisers and the organ of communication between the people and the management. Obtaining in this way a great influence over their ignorant and credulous countrymen, they readily and without difficulty instilled into them the same prejudices and jealousies with which they themselves were possessed.'

But on the whole, Loch was able to report, the ignorant and credulous country people had shown a remarkable resistance to so many evil influences. The advantages of the improvements were indeed obvious enough to any unbiased person. 'It seemed as if it had been pointed out by Nature, that the system for this remote district, in order that it might bear its suitable importance in contributing its share to the general stock of the country, was to convert the mountainous districts into sheep-walks, and to remove the inhabitants to the coast, or to the valleys near the sea.' These requirements of the national economy were carefully explained to the ignorant and credulous people of Sutherland and Strathnaver 'by the factor personally, or by written statements communicated to them by the ground officers'. Such men would have required interpreters, which is what Loch means when he continues: 'That nothing might be ommitted in this respect, the different ministers, and the principal tacksmen connected with the districts which were to be newly arranged, were written to, explaining to them fully and explicitly the intentions of the proprietors in adopting them. It was particularly requested of these gentlemen that they would impress upon the minds of the people the propriety of agreeing to them.'

James Loch had reached the seventy-fifth page of his account. The motives of the promoters of Celtic darkness had been exposed, and now at last the ministers of God were depicted in their pulpits, translating the message of English benevolence into Gaelic for the edification of their flocks. Loch had at length come to the moment of actual conflict between the forces of advancing civilization and those of selfishness and ignorance. 'These representations had the desired effect, and nothing can be more praiseworthy, or deserve more to be applauded, than the conduct of the people on quitting their original habitations: for although they left them with much regret, they did so in the most quiet, orderly and peaceable manner.'

It is a most astonishing anti-climax.

Loch seems to have felt, too, that it contained an apparent inconsistency with the circumstances of Sellar's trial four years earlier, for he added this explanation. 'If, upon one occasion in the earlier years of these arrangements, a momentary feeling of a contrary nature was exhibited, it arose entirely from the misconduct of persons whose duty it was to have recommended and enforced obedience to the laws, in place of infusing into the minds of the people feelings of a contrary description. As soon, however, as the interference of these persons was withdrawn, the poor people returned to their usual state of quietness and repose.' The mystery behind Sellar's trial was finally dissipated: William Chisholm and others had been put up to their tricks by Sheriff Mackid, and once he had been removed there was no further trouble.

In the years following Sellar's acquittal, the benevolence of the factors and the philanthropy of Lord and Lady Stafford were spurred to speedier well-doing than before. There were crop failures in 1816–17, and 'in order to alleviate this misery, every exertion was made by Lord Stafford. To those who had cattle he advanced money to the amount of above THREE THOUSAND POUNDS. To supply those who had no cattle he sent meal into the country to the amount of nearly NINE THOUSAND POUNDS. Besides which, Lady STAFFORD distributed money to each parish on the estate.'

Then a typhus epidemic ravaged Strathnaver through the years 1818 and 1819. 'As soon as this circumstance was known, every pains possible were taken by the proprietors to arrest its progress, and prevent the contagion spreading. Directions, besides, were given to send from Apothecaries' hall three large parcels of Peruvian bark and calomel, which was thankfully received by the people, and tended to check the disease and restrain its ravages.'

Such dreadful by-products of the former pattern of society on the Sutherland estate acted as a strong incentive to hasten the plan of improvement, and to them was added another. 'Upon examining acccurately the names of those claiming relief, with the rentals and other lists, it appeared that a very numerous body had fixed themselves in the more remote districts of the estate, and on the outskirts of the more distant towns, who held neither of landlord nor of any tacksmen; and who, in short, enjoyed the benefit of residing upon the property without paying *any rent whatever*. Their numbers amounted to no less than FOUR HUNDRED AND EIGHT FAMILIES, consisting of nearly TWO THOUSAND individuals.' Loch's statement that these people 'had fixed themselves' in such inaccessible parts of the estate that they remained unnoticed until hunger drove them forth suggests that they were part of the redundant population of the earlier improvements. It was indeed surprising that so many people could have survived the rigours of successive winters among the bleak recesses of the northern hills. 'But this fact having been once discovered, it certainly would have been most unreasonable to expect that steps should not have been taken to remedy this evil, by removing the whole of these people to the coast, and by adopting such rules as would prevent, in future, the settlement of a similar class upon the property.'

But Loch had still not exhausted the excellent reasons why the improvement plan was implemented so rapidly between 1816 and 1820. 'As long as the people remained in the hills, in the fear of being removed, their habits would necessarily have become more desultory and less industrious than they even naturally were. Nor was it possible, to expect from people so situated, the punctual payment of their rents, and nothing could be more certain than that they would take every advantage of the land of which they knew they were not long to continue to be occupiers.' The inscrutability of this passage is soon clarified. 'The necessity of completing' the clearances 'as speedily as possible was called for also, in consequence of the serious and extensive losses experienced by the stock-farmers: amounting in each year to many hundred sheep. By them these losses were invariably and without exception ascribed to the depredations of the Highlanders.'

Disease, starvation, refugees paying no rent, danger to property, were the manifold evils which could all be cured at once by the removal of the natives. 'It was determined therefore, that the whole of the removals should be completed in the month of May, of the years 1819 and 1820, respectively, and notice to that effect was given, so far back as in the autumn of 1817.'[3]

In addition to such long notice, extraordinary concessions were offered to the Highlanders. They could occupy their former homes for a year rent-free provided they moved without delay. The estate would pay the value of their bog-fir to save them the trouble of carrying it to their new sites, and provide timber for them there. It would advance money to enable them to buy a boat. But once again the poor ignorant people 'were encouraged by those who expected, that if they could get the people to hold out to the last, they would force their landlords to abandon their arrangements; thus, as is always the case with such advisers, sacrificing the interest of the people to their own selfish purposes'.

But Loch was able to cite one community, living about eight miles from the coast up the Naver valley, whose behaviour was exemplary. It consisted 'of the people of Dunviden, and of other towns in the heights of Strathnaver, who, in order to facilitate a particular arrangement, agreed to quit their places in May 1818, and settled in their new lots at Strathy with the utmost cheerfulness. They were rewarded for this conduct, by obtaining a present of their seed corn.'

James Loch could scarcely have instanced a more striking example of co-operation. For the people of Dunviden had already been removed from the upper end of the Naver valley only four years earlier, in circumstances described during the trial of Patrick Sellar (see ante, page seven). Having dug fresh ground and built themselves new homes, they could hardly have welcomed the reappearance of Patrick Sellar himself with a fresh mandate to remove them again. But according to James Loch the people of Dunviden were eager enough to continue playing their part in the still expanding improvements, and well might he castigate the disloyalty of those whose loyalty had been less severely tested.

As for the new allotments on the coast, it was important that they should not be too large. 'Indeed, if they had been so, one great object of the arrangement would have been entirely lost: for if the people had subsisted altogether or chiefly on their lots, they never would have gone much to sea. Or if, on the other hand, they became active fishermen, their lots must have been imperfectly cultivated.'

Other thoughtful measures in addition to the ideal size of the allotments were devised for the protection of the people, particularly against the defects in their own characters. For Loch found the Gaels to be the victims of 'every species of deceit and idleness, by which they contracted habits and ideas, quite incompatible with the customs of regular society, and civilized life, adding greatly to those defects which characterize persons living in a loose and unformed state of society'. One example of this was their propensity for taking fish from the rivers of Strathnaver. 'The principal rivers are of considerable value as salmon fishings, and have been let at a proportional rent to Berwick fish salesmen. In order to protect this property, and to preserve the breed of this valuable fish, strict orders were given to prevent the rivers being poached upon at any time, but especially during the close season. It was difficult to convince the people that such a regulation was meant to be effectual; for the habits already described rendered such a pursuit one of their chief employments, and the checking it almost appeared to them to be interfering with a vested right.'

The people also suffered from a habit of early marriage, 'a principle in every respect most praiseworthy, and which strongly upholds the moral character of a people, when the subsistence of the family is obtained through the exertion and labour of the parents. But when their maintenance must be left to the gratuitous support of others, it degenerates into a selfish gratification of passion.' However, Loch did not profess to have decided yet what was the proper solution to this particular evil of 'a redundant population'.

But he looked forward to the future with profound optimism. 'In a few years the character of the whole of this population will be completely changed. . . . The children of those who are removed from the hills will lose all recollection of the habits and customs of their fathers.' Already the transformation was plain to see. 'It is a fact of the most gratifying nature to be enabled to state, that the conduct and behaviour of these people, as well as of all the others upon the coast, have become gradually more steady and correct, in proportion as they have become more

24

industrious. The bare mention of such facts is sufficient to show the importance of these works to the country in every point of view, and the rapid progress which the people have already made. Can there be a more convincing proof of the efficacy of that line of conduct, which has produced such an admirable effect?'

All that remained was to extend such blessings to the furthest possible limits. Of the 800,000 Scottish acres of the Sutherland estate 'the only hill districts which are still occupied, in some degree, according to the old system are the small farm of Knockin and Elphin in Assynt, the district near Lairg, the lower part of Strathfleet, and the district round the Kirk of Rogart. . . . How far upon the general expiration of the tacks in 1828 a new arrangement of a portion of these people may be necessary will require much deliberation.' Meanwhile the chief of clan Mackay, Lord Reay, still owned most of Strathnaver, to the extent of nearly half a million Scottish acres, and the philanthropists of Dunrobin could plan no new enterprises on the scale of those James Loch described unless there was a change of ownership.

Of all who could share the credit for these remarkable improvements, none could claim it more directly than Elizabeth Gordon, Countess of Sutherland. The Marquess of Stafford had certainly contributed to them generously from his English fortune, while James Loch had perfected and executed the master plan. But the Countess-Marchioness was *Ban-mhorair Chataibh*, the Great Lady of Sutherland, and as all the peoples on her estates looked to her to protect the society of which she was the head, so they would address their petitions to her when they felt aggrieved, and their gratitude to her when they received benefits.

James Loch went so far as to describe the Countess as of Celtic descent, but in this he exaggerated. The Gordons were of Lowland origin, and Elizabeth Gordon possessed a background similar to his own. She had been born and brought up in Edinburgh, and had spent a considerable time in London also before she first set eyes on Dunrobin Castle at the age of seventeen.

But she was the Great Lady of Sutherland nevertheless, and there can be no doubt of the sense of responsibility she felt for the reputation of her position in the very un-Celtic world in which she lived. In 1819 she wrote a letter to a friend from her husband's palace of Trentham in Staffordshire, enclosing the earlier account of the Sutherland improvements which Loch expanded into the volume of 1820. 'We have lately been much attacked in the newspapers,' the Great Lady of Sutherland was driven to complain, 'by a few malicious writers who have long assailed us on every occasion. What is stated is most perfectly unjust and unfounded, as I am convinced from the facts I am acquainted with; and I venture to trouble you with the enclosed note, as a sort of statement of our proceedings, though with some scruple in plaguing you with what to you must be a bore—only if you meet with discussions on the subject in society, I shall be glad if you will show this statement to anyone who may interest him or herself on the subject.' So one of the richest women in Europe was forced to defend herself, using subterfuge, against the slanders of a remote people who could not even understand the language in which Society discussed them.

But if she hoped that James Loch's Account would silence the malicious critics she had not long to wait for a most bitter disappointment.

3

What the Englishman Said
1820

————◆••••◆————

A T Spring Vale near Stone in Staffordshire a native of that
country read the Account of James Loch, and such was the
energy engendered by his indignation that he had composed a
reply of 148 pages and seen it through the Press by the same
summer of 1820 in which Loch's own work was offered for sale.

His name was Thomas Bakewell, and the property of which
he was tenant did not lie upon the Staffordshire estates of the
Marquess and Marchioness. It must have required courage,
even so, to write as he did about the factor of such immensely
powerful neighbours, and Bakewell seems to have been moved
to do so primarily by his concern for the reputation of Lord
Stafford and of those who comprised the great rural family of his
estate of Trentham. He prefaced his remarks by a personal
letter to James Loch himself.

'I have for a long time given indulgence to a painful feeling
which is, I believe, common to some thousands of the natives of
Staffordshire; and as you are by many supposed to be the sole
cause, I think it but right to inform you of it.

'It is well known that the late Marquess of Stafford was a
very popular character. . . . It is thought that he commanded
or influenced the choice of more Members of Parliament than
any other Nobleman in England: yet such was his popularity
amongst the most numerous classes of society that a murmur
was scarcely heard.

'You may recollect that about six or seven years ago you

told me, that the present Marquess of Stafford was fully aware of the value of popularity, as a means of avoiding much evil, and of doing much good in society; and that, as his Lordship's Agent, you considered it your duty to observe that line of conduct which should effectually secure his popularity. If such were your sentiments, and I have no reason to doubt it, what a strange dereliction there has been from a known duty. I have not heard of one single act being ascribed to your Agency that was in the least degree calculated to make Lord Stafford popular, while common rumour has been continually reporting acts of yours which were sure to make him unpopular, and even hated; and it is reported too, that Lord Stafford's pecuniary interests have been greatly injured by those measures which have rendered him so very unpopular. . . .

'For the reports about the transactions in Sutherlandshire I constantly expressed my incredulity as to the leading features of them, till I read your published defence of those transactions; this defence, while it entirely removed incredulity, placed the leading features of the case more fully in view and heightened the complexion of them, like an unskilful painter, who while he is defending some detected defect in his picture, throws a more glaring light upon it.'

It is sufficiently strange that the affairs of distant Sutherland should have excited Bakewell or anyone else in Staffordshire. But there is no cause to doubt Bakewll's report on the measure of this interest: it merely corroborates what the Countess of Sutherland and James Loch had already reported. 'I beg to say,' Thomas Bakewell wrote once he had proceeded to his *Remarks*, 'that I speak of nothing but what the world speaks of; I am in a situation to hear the good as well as the bad, and I trust that I am as much disposed to relate the former as the latter. I make no doubt but there has been much exaggeration; indeed I know there has been some, and this will always be the case when the tide of popular odium sets in; still I believe that truth will bear us out in some very unpleasant reflections.'

But Thomas Bakewell possessed a sense of humour as marked as James Loch's sense of the immanence of devils, and the native of Staffordshire leavened his unpleasant reflections with facetiousness almost to the extent that the man of Edinburgh subdued his tale of triumph with conjurations. It was unfortunate for Loch that Bakewell's mirth in sorrow made so much better reading than his own gloom-laden jubilations.

'The readers of Mr. Loch's publication may feast their imaginations on wonders,' Bakewell told the public. 'The admirable Crichton was a Scotchman, too, and till now I thought the tales about him fabulous; but incredulity is completely put to the blush, for we have living proofs of living wonders in this book: the highest exploits of Crichton fall short of the rapid improvements produced by the magic wand of Mr. Loch.

'The poet says, "slow and easy; they stumble who go fast": but Mr. Loch never stumbles, no impediments stop his way, no checks prevent his progress, nor cause one retrogade movement. Look at what Sutherland was a few years back—an almost pathless wilderness, no carriages of any kind could be dragged through it, nor human beings pass, except by single files and at a slow pace. The country swarming with that dirty, slothful and mischievous animal man, living in filthy huts, inferior to the hogsties of other countries; the land uncultivated, in which only barren wastes and impassable bogs and morasses contended for pre-eminence; while lochs, straths and burns abounded with fish, yet the people being too ignorant and too lazy to catch them, would all starve were it not for the unparalleled bounty of their Lord. Mr. Loch passes over it in double quick time—"he came, he saw, he overcame": his eye, like the bright luminary of day, darts its rays upon the sides of the mountains, pierces the deep glens, and peeps through the rafters of these filthy hovels, and sees men, their wives and dirty bairns, their cows, pigs, dogs, cats, and a great variety of vermin, all inhabiting the same apartment. His first object is to drive out that master-piece of sloth and uselessness—man and all his retinue. The huts are destroyed; the smoke of the burning moss timber quickly mingles with the clouds. The potato patches are soon converted into beautiful pasture grounds. . . .'

Bakewell next considered Loch's random statements on an important question: who had actually originated the policy he described? 'How adroitly does he avoid that egotism which is so hateful to an enlightened mind. In almost every page we hear of the Marquess or the Marchioness—Lord and Lady Stafford, the proprietor or the landlord having done this or that to promote the comfort and happiness of their people, when it is well known to be Mr. Loch himself that has done all these great things.'

There seems to have been a widespread opinion, shared by Bakewell, that Lord Stafford was a fundamentally good man, given to 'reserve and seclusion'. His unpopularity could only be caused by the freedom which James Loch enjoyed to act in his name. Bakewell took great trouble to expound this delicate matter. 'What most forcibly struck me,' he remarked by way of anecdote, 'and to which I attach much importance, was the spontaneous and warm expression of a gentleman of great respectability, who must know Lord Stafford's real disposition better than any other man, and he is a person of no mean attainments in the knowledge of the human heart. . . . I had been speaking to him upon the Sutherlandshire affair, and saying that the statements intended to exculpate those implicated in the charges were by no means satisfactory, and tended to confirm them, which he appeared unable to controvert; but evidently with agitated feelings, he said, "Well, I will never believe that Lord Stafford is in the least capable of doing anything cruel or unjust, knowing it to be such; but like every other man, his Lordship is liable to be deceived by misrepresentations." '
Bakewell said nothing about Lady Stafford, however, and it is difficult to interpret his silence other than ominously.

At page 81 Bakewell remarked, 'it is time to be serious, for much serious matter lies before us', and at this point the levity disappears from his analysis. He addressed himself first to the question of the numbers affected by the Sutherland evictions, a matter Loch had not thought it sufficiently important to mention. The original number on the estate had been 'stated at fifteen thousand, scattered we may suppose over the whole of it, some as landholders or tacksmen, others as small farmers, and many as poor cottagers. It is determined to turn all the interior into large sheep farms, and in consequence all the inhabitants not connected with this new order of things are ejected from their homes. A part of these settle upon the sea coast in places appointed for the purpose, and betake themselves to a new and perilous mode of life as fishers. Another part emigrate to the sickly woods of America, and another part remove to the more hospitable hills of two neighbouring counties. So far is perfectly clear from Mr. Loch's own statement, but he does not inform us what numbers were ejected. We are left to suppose it was many thousands, but have no means of telling how many. For what purpose does Mr. Loch omit stating their actual numbers; in other things he is extremely particular in his details, why is he not the same in this?'

Bakewell turned next to the new allotments. 'Another thing wants explaining; it is said that all the people removed by eject-ment might have settled upon lots appointed for them. Yet in another part it is represented that all the lots marked out have been taken up. We may ask then, is the new population of Brora, Strathnaver and parts adjacent entirely made up of those removed from the interior of Lord Stafford's estate, or is it part made up from discarded sailors and soldiers, or such others as were glad to obtain a settlement anywhere?' Bakewell has here overlooked the good character and conduct clause which was so fundamental to the issue of Sellar's trial, but this is not surpris-ing, because James Loch (whether by accident or design) had done the very same.

And now Thomas Bakewell explored some of the reasoning with which James Loch had justified his system of improvement. 'We are informed that Lord Stafford was not the first to act upon this scheme of depopulating large districts for the sake of extensive sheep farms, for that others have previously acted upon it, particularly Lord Reay and others in the same county, and yet their doing so had not been productive of murmurs or clamour amongst the people, or the invidious reflections of others.[4] Now, if the measure requires an apology, and this passage appears to admit that it does, what apology can it be for one of the most opulent noblemen in England, if not in Europe, doing that which is wrong, because those less opulent and less conspicuous in life had done it before him? And if the inhabitants of the other estates in the same county had been removed with-out murmur, and the removal of those upon Lord Stafford's estates did cause murmurs and reflections, and indeed severe censures, is it not a strong argument that there was a difference in the manner of doing it?'

Bakewell did not summarize the passage in which Loch had spoken of the strong attachment of the Gaels for the homes and customs of their ancestors, and of their reluctance to part with such unprogressive emotions. He quoted it verbatim, and added: 'For what purpose, in the name of humanity and common propriety was the above beautiful passage written and published by Mr. Loch? Was it to show with what ease he could trample upon the prejudices and local attachments of the lowest class of society? The stronger local attachment of the poor than the rich is an admitted fact.'

Thomas Bakewell's manner was by this time very different from the facetious, bantering tone of his earlier pages. Anger and contempt for this pretentious busybody from Edinburgh had begun to simmer in this private English countryman of Staffordshire. His charges had all been intuitive, for he knew nothing of the Gaelic peoples of Sutherland, and his only weapon was that he had perceived that James Loch really knew no more about them than he did. He also believed him capable of deliberate deceit, and this was the issue of his next question.

'In Mr. Loch's letter it is mentioned too that Lord Stafford had from time to time extended his relief to these poor improvident Highlanders, and to the amount of ten thousand pounds in one year; and in his publication it is stated that in one winter of great distress nine thousand pounds' worth of meal had been furnished to them. Now it is a fair question, was this meal given to them, or was it sold at an under price? We might suppose the former, from the wording of both statements. Was it not sold at a saving price, if not a price of profit, and the amount taken in cattle or other moveables; or, if in part sold upon credit, were not the debts so incurred afterwards stated in the account of moss timber against them?'

It was not merely a question whether Loch had been claiming a vast scheme of philanthropy when there had been none. The moss timber was in question, the only part of a highland dwelling that remained the property of an evicted tenant. The horrid rumours of wholesale arson of dwelling-houses to force people to leave had not been scotched by the acquittal of Patrick Sellar in 1816. But Loch had explained the whole misunderstanding on which they were based. Outgoing tenants had been paid for their bog timber by the landlord to save them the trouble of carrying it with them, while fresh timber had awaited them at their allotments. The old bog timber, being useless to the landlord, had been burned on the spot. Bakewell suggested a very different explanation: the landlord's price had been paid when he gave food to starving people and thereby earned the right to burn the only material in all that land with which they were entitled to build themselves a roof. It was indeed a serious charge, and one that would have to be answered.

But whatever the true circumstances of what had occurred in that remote corner of Britain, it was at least agreed that a human population had been removed to make room for sheep, 'and it does certainly seem as if these large sheep farms were the primary object, and not the ameliorating the condition of man in the transaction alluded to. It may be very pleasing to the eye of fancy to see far extended glens and mountain sides under a beautiful verdure and numerous flocks of sheep, joined to the pride of ownership; and in fancy to count the gains of this mode of farming, and to have that animal, man, far removed. But these feelings are exclusively the privilege of those interested: the feelings of others will intuitively be led to regret and deprecate the misery that must be the consequence. It seems most strange that any individual, the subject of a free state, should venture upon a measure of such magnitude. We have heard of conquerors doing such things; we have never heard of the legislature attempting anything of the kind, much less, till lately, did we ever hear of private individuals removing by force whole communities.'

Thomas Bakewell spoke of the responsibility of Parliament to investigate, but cut himself short with the reflection: 'We may at least suspend that expectation; and it may rather be presumed that the late duty upon imported wool may have reference to these extensive and increasing sheep-walks in the Highlands of Scotland.' At this time Parliament was dominated by landowners.

No doubt they had benefited by the change, 'for some will be benefited by any change; and in the affair of Sutherlandshire, the good and happiness that has been produced by the change may be estimated. But no one is able to estimate the evil that may have been produced by it; no one can say how many have been made miserable for life by it; no one can tell how many premature deaths may have been occasioned by it.'

In conclusion, Bakewell remarked on Loch's advocacy of his own cause. 'If all these fine things are as this writer states, why does not someone else state them? But many things are done that cannot be undone, and that it would be much better to bury in oblivion: at any rate to suffer the impressions made by them to be weakened by time, and opposite conduct, instead of attempting to blazon them forth and gloss them over by sophistry.' Bakewell was misunderstanding the statement in Loch's introductory letter to his employers, that the measures he described had been completed. This did not mean that James Loch and his masters had no further plans of the same sort, not by any means.

It seems unlikely that Bakewell's *Remarks* achieved a wide circulation, except perhaps in Staffordshire, and there is no evidence that the Marquess or Marchioness ever set eyes on it. An Englishman in his position could hardly have carried much weight as an authority on Scottish matters in comparison with James Loch, and this seems to have been in his mind when he observed: 'I cannot have the least apprehension of doing Mr. Loch any disservice, for I cannot suppose that anything I shall say will at all shake the stability of that extensive patronage he is honoured with.' He had nevertheless gone to great trouble, probably to expense, and possibly to personal danger, to express his sympathy for human beings whom he believed to be in grave distress.

If any of his words caused Loch alarm, it may have been these: 'He may think himself very fortunate indeed if he meet no antagonist more formidable than myself.' But what kind of reader of the newly published Account could prove formidable? He would have to be a Highlander with the real knowledge of Gaeldom that Loch himself lacked. Yet he would have to be a gentleman of respectable family, whose motives in criticizing the factor of a great landlord could not be questioned. His activities and his acquaintance would have to be of the most influential kind. . . .

Just such a person was already studying James Loch's Account of the improvements in Sutherland, with less haste but no less anger.

4

What the General Said
1822

———◆◆◆———

O<small>N</small> the 24th April 1821 David Stewart of Garth wrote his short preface to the book in which he had distilled the experience of a busy life in the crucible of nearly four years' labour. It was entitled *Sketches of the Character, Manners, and Present State of the Highlanders of Scotland: with Details of the Military Service of the Highland Regiments*, and such a long title was not unseemly for the masterpiece of over a thousand pages which it described.

David Stewart had returned from the Napoleonic war in 1815, after serving with the 42nd Highlanders, or the Black Watch, in many theatres since 1787. He had been placed on half-pay with the rank of Colonel and created a Commander of the Order of the Bath. But perhaps the honour that gave him the greatest satisfaction was the one his Commander-in-Chief, the Duke of York, bestowed upon his regiment. Colonel Stewart was a vice-president of the Highland Society in London and the Duke of York himself was the President who in 1817 made a presentation to the Black Watch 'in token of the respect of the Society for a corps which, for more than seventy years had contributed to uphold the martial character of their country'. And it was this association between Colonel Stewart and the son of the King that led to the composition of his great work, for the Commander-in-Chief directed that the 42nd Regiment should draw up a record of its services, and in 1817 David Stewart was invited to undertake the task.

In the veteran soldier's portrait the military uniform contrasts with a scholar's gentle expression, in which the eyes gaze placidly through spectacles beneath a high brow fringed with white hair. He was described as a man of middle height and of a robust frame much impaired by wounds received in action. This man had been brought up to be bilingual in a Gaelic society near the southernmost boundary of Celtic Scotland, and descended from Robert II King of Scots through his second son the Earl of Buchan. The Earl's son Alexander had built Garth castle in Perthshire a little after 1390, and as Colonel Stewart recorded, 'there are now living in the district of Athole, within its ancient boundary, 1835 persons of the name of Stewart, descendants of this man in the male line, besides numbers in other parts of the kingdom'.

Returning to the country that he knew and loved so well, David Stewart found that he could not confine his study to his own regiment or his own district: he could not describe the lives of his comrades in war without relating them to the home backgrounds in which their standards of conduct had been learned: he could not relate present events without reference to the past. 'Hence I have been led on, step by step, from one attempt to another, till the whole attained its present form. . . . I trust, therefore, that from the enlightened reader who . . . reflects on the difficulties which a plain soldier, unaccustomed to composition, had to encounter in making such an attempt as that now respectfully, and with great diffidence, submitted to the Public, I shall meet with that liberal share of indulgence which I so much require.'

He was not disappointed. The expensive two-volume edition appeared in 1822 and was instantly sold out. The same year a second edition was issued in which Stewart was able to write: 'I have been farther gratified by receiving numerous communications, confirming the general correctness of the great multiplicity of facts and circumstances which I have had occasion to detail.' The author inherited Garth at this time, on the death of his brother, and in August he was called to Edinburgh for the visit of George IV, where he acted as adviser to Sir Walter Scott in Highland matters.

The second edition sold out as rapidly as the first, but before the third was prepared David Stewart spent three months in

1823 during which he travelled about a thousand miles through the Highlands, checking the accuracy of his own work. 'If I have seen cause to make but few alterations, with hardly a qualification, even in those economical views which are of course most liable to be disputed, it is solely because the result of the most minute enquiries, and of personal observation, has strikingly confirmed the general accuracy of my statements and reasonings, and affords me additional confidence in the truth and justness of the opinions which I was previously led to maintain.' It was 1825 before this third edition appeared, the year in which David Stewart of Garth was promoted Major-General.

His book, the most comprehensive social study of Celtic Scotland that had ever been made by a single author, began by distinguishing the two separate peoples of his little country. 'For seven centuries Birnam Hill, at the entrance into Athol, has formed the boundary between the Lowlands and Highlands, and between the Saxon and Gaelic languages. On the south and east sides of the hill, breeches are worn and the Scotch Lowland dialect spoken with as broad an accent as in Mid-Lothian. On the north and west sides are found the Gaelic, the kilt and the plaid, with all the peculiarities of the Highland character.' Stewart shunned the vague and sweeping statement, and built his thesis on such minute examples as this.

He next explained Celtic Scotland as the refuge of a people who had been for centuries resisting the 'oppressions and the dominion of a more powerful neighbour. Thus, in the absence of their monarchs, and defended by their barrier of rocks, they did not always submit to the authority of a distant government which could neither enforce obedience nor afford protection.' A patriarchal system bound them in many separate societies; of whose virtues and defects Stewart gave diverse examples. He described how an evil Stewart of Garth had been imprisoned in a cell of the castle by his own kindred in about 1520, and he was able to contrast this anecdote with another from Breadalbane, where in more recent times there had been no appeal to the law in fifty-five years. For better or worse, this patriarchal jurisdiction in the Highlands had been abolished. Speaking of the Duke of Atholl's court of regality at Logierait, Stewart remarked: 'The hall in which the feudal parliament assembled (a noble chamber of better proportions than the British House of

Commons) has been pulled down, and one of the most conspicuous vestiges of the almost regal influence of this powerful
family has thus been destroyed.'

But the Highlanders had retained a deep loyalty to one
another and to their chiefs, as the aftermath of the Forty-Five
had proved. They had retained a deep love for their home-acre:
and here Stewart could not resist telling the story of an old
woman of ninety-one who had walked to the Lowlands to visit
her daughter the previous winter. When it began to snow she
had slipped out of the house during the night and walked home,
for if she had stayed much longer 'and if I had died, they could
not have sent my remains home through the deep snows. If I
had told my daughter, perhaps she would have locked the door
upon me, and God forbid that my bones should be at such a
distance from home, and be buried among *Gall na machair*—the
strangers of the plain.'

Pride of kindred was nourished by the heroic poetry and
tales of the land, and love of country had recently given utter-
ance to one of the finest outpourings of nature poetry in
European literature. 'When a boy I took great pleasure in
hearing these recitations, and now reflect with much surprise on
the ease and rapidity with which a person could continue them
for hours, without hesitation and without stopping, except to
give the argument or prelude to a new chapter or subject. One
of the most remarkable of these reciters in my time was Duncan
Macintyre, a native of Glenlyon in Perthshire, who died in
September 1816, in his 93rd year.'[*] Stewart recorded with
satisfaction that the Highland Society of London had settled a
small pension on Duncan Macintyre towards the end of his days.

Stewart felt obliged to mention another theme of Gaelic verse
and story-telling. 'The demure solemnity and fanaticism of the
plains unluckily offered a ceaseless subject of ridicule and satire
to the poetical imaginations of the mountaineers. The truth is,
that no two classes of people of the same country, and in such
close neighbourhood, could possibly present a greater contrast.
. . . Differing so widely in their manners, they heartily
despised and hated each other.' At no point in his book did
Stewart pay either Patrick Sellar or James Loch the compliment

[*] *The Songs of Duncan Ban Macintyre*, Ed. Angus Macleod, 1952. The poet was
born in 1724 and died in 1812.

of mentioning them by name, but he took this early opportunity of explaining that the contempt and hatred they had so recently expressed in print for his countrymen was heartily reciprocated.

One of the chief dangers now menacing Celtic society in Scotland was the change in relationship between the landlord, once the trusted and respected head of a family, and his tenants who still considered themselves to be members of it. Sometimes this was caused by Highland landlords going over to the Englishry, sometimes by sale of estates to strangers. 'Land-lords are thus deprived of the power of holding that free and confidential communication with their tenants which is necessary to acquire a knowledge of their character, disposition, and talents. Trusting therefore to interpreters, and without any immediate communication, much misconception and often dis-tress to the tenant ensue, as well as frequent misapprehension and prejudiced notions of their character and turn of thinking on the part of the landlord.'

In those areas of the Highlands of which the landlords were now absentee aliens, the presence of the tacksmen, or gentlemen farmers with large tenant holdings, was all the more essential to preserve the local standards and amenities of social life. 'The rank and influence which these respectable men held are now void, their places being, in most cases, filled up by shepherds and graziers from the south, or by such natives as had stock or credit to undertake their farms. This new class being generally without birth, education, or any of the qualifications requisite to secure the respect of the people on those great estates, where there are no resident proprietors, the inhabitants are left without a man of talent, or of sufficient influence, from rank or education, to settle the most ordinary disputes, or capable of acting as a justice of the peace, and of signing those certificates and affidavits which the law in so many instances requires.' Sellar had spoken sarcastically of the country that now lay under his sheep reposing under the domination of 'old half-pay officers and other tacksmen' (p. 14). Stewart saw the matter differently.

It was necessary at this point to analyse the social and economic revolution that was taking place in the Highlands, and in doing so Stewart turned Loch's exposition on the same subject inside out without directly referring to it. Loch had described his policy in Sutherland as the extension to a barbarous region

39

of the improvements in agriculture long adopted in the more civilized Lowlands. His exposition was both in style and content that of a townsman brought up in Edinburgh and educated in the law in London. Stewart brought to his analysis of the systems of the Highlands and the Lowlands the experience of his upbringing on a progressive estate near the border of the two regions, together with his gift for relevant detail.

The Lowland systems were indeed far advanced in practice, compared with Highland systems as he described them, but not so advanced in time as some thought. 'It was not till after the year 1770 that Mr. John White, at Kirkton of Mailler in Strathearn, first introduced the green crop system into Perthshire. The farmer who first commenced the system of dry fallow in East Lothian only died in this reign. This new mode of agriculture was considered so extraordinary that for some time it was looked upon as the result of a disordered intellect, even in the now highly cultivated district of the Lothians.' Stewart was eager that those agricultural improvements of the Lowlands which were applicable to the Highlands should be extended to them, and he devoted considerable space to suggestions about the best methods of doing this.

But he did not mince words over the methods used by William Young, Patrick Sellar, and James Loch. 'Had the Lothian gentlemen of that period ejected the bulk of the ancient inhabitants as ignorant, prejudiced, indolent and without capital, placing those who were allowed to remain on barren and detached patches of land; and had they invited strangers from England, France, Flanders, or whoever would offer the best rent, would there not have been the same senseless clamour (as the expression of the indignant feelings, roused by various measures pursued in the Highlands, is called)?' This passage, like many that have been quoted already from Stewart's book, is taken from a footnote. It is evident that the author had almost completed his thesis before Loch's *Account* was published in 1820, and that these footnotes often reveal the feelings with which he studied it.

Even supposing, Stewart argued, that such methods of improvement were right, either for the Highlands or for Britain as a whole, 'improvements in which so few of the people were to have a share; conciliatory measures, and a degree of tenderness beyond what would have been shown to strangers were to have been expected towards the hereditary supporters of their families. It was, however, unfortunately the natural consequences of the measures which were adopted, that few men of liberal feelings could be induced to undertake their execution. The respectable gentlemen who, in so many cases, had formerly been entrusted with the management of Highland property resigned, and their places were supplied by persons cast in a coarser mould, and generally strangers to the country who, detesting the people, and ignorant of their character, capability and language, quickly surmounted every obstacle, and hurried on the change, without reflecting on the distress of which it might be productive.'

Stewart was a Highland landlord of royal descent who understood and reverenced the deep feelings of loyalty he enjoyed. To have abused such loyalty was in his eyes the behaviour of a savage, 'where a gradual, prudent and proper change would not have excited riots among a people distinguished for their hereditary obedience to their superiors, nor rendered it necessary to eject them from their possessions by force, or, as in some instances, by burning their houses over their heads and driving them out, homeless and unsheltered, to the open heath'.

In this passage he had repeated categorically the charge of arson of dwelling-houses dismissed by an Inverness jury to the satisfaction of an Edinburgh judge and subsequently denied in Loch's *Account*. Stewart consequently felt it necessary to insist on the reliability of his evidence before he had proceeded much further. 'It is painful to dwell on this subject, but as information, communicated by men of honour, judgment and perfect veracity, descriptive of what they daily witness, affords the best means of forming a correct judgment, and as these gentlemen, from their situations in life, have no immediate interest in the determination of the question beyond what is dictated by humanity and a love of truth, their authority may be considered as undoubted.'[5]

Stewart turned his attention to the lives of the people affected by the policy of improvement. 'It is certain,' said the man who had fought in Flanders and the West Indies, Minorca, Egypt, and Spain, 'that there is no recent instance in which so much unmerited suffering has produced so little compassion. The cruelty of removing the slaves on a West India estate to one perhaps scarcely five miles distant, is frequently reprobated in the strongest terms. Yet we find the ejectment or emigration of the Highlanders viewed with apathy, and their feelings of despair deemed unworthy of notice. . . . A very honourable and humane friend of mine, who has exerted himself powerfully in the cause of the poor negroes, told me not long ago, and was not well pleased because I would not coincide in his opinion, that Sutherland contained 20,000 inhabitants too many, and that that they ought to be removed without delay, and sent to the colonies.'

The condition of Highlanders removed in this way was indeed not unlike that of the negro. 'As two-thirds of these people are unable to pay for their passage, they must bind themselves to serve for a term of years the person who pays for them, and who again disposes of them to the highest bidder; a species of slavery not very agreeable to the dispositions of the mountaineers.'

In describing the manner of removal Stewart referred to the report of Patrick Sellar's trial, and permitted himself a direct attack on the character of the Great Lady of Sutherland. 'The trial ended (as was expected by every person who understood the circumstances) in the acquittal of the acting agent, the verdict of the jury proceeding on the principle that he acted under legal authority. This acquittal, however, did by no means diminish the general feeling of culpability; it only transferred the offence from the agent to a quarter too high and too distant to be directly affected by public indignation, if indeed there be any station so elevated or so distant that public indignation, justly excited, will not sooner or later reach, so as to touch the feelings however obtuse of the transgressor of that law of humanity written on every upright mind.'

Not merely had the people of Sutherland and parts of Strathnaver been deprived of their homes: they had been deprived of their reputations also by sytematic defamation. It was said that they were a burden to their landlord, preserved from starvation only by his private philanthropy. In fact, the people of that land had maintained a family of earls in considerable state for over twenty generations, 'a length of succession unparalleled in the peerage of this country'. As for the much-publicized charity, it was a hoax, as Bakewell had suspected. 'It has been stated that the starving population have been relieved by remittances to the amount of several thousand pounds in money, grain and meal; but it was not said that good security (or cattle) was taken for payment of this relief, and that, except in cases of great destitution, where all property had been previously disposed of to resist a similar calamity, the whole remittances were paid up.' As to whether the people had been living in destitution before the improvements began, statistics were available to disprove this. 'On reference to the poor's funds, taken on an average of many years previous to 1800, it will be found that in those days, when that country was so populous that this formed one of the alleged causes of removal, the sums paid to the poor of this surplus population in the parish of Rogart, containing 2023 persons, were under £13 annually: in the parish of Farr, containing 2408 persons, under £12: in Assynt, containing 2395 inhabitants, under £11: in Kildonan, containing 1443 persons, under £8 annually. Other parishes were nearly in the same proportion, and at this moderate expense were all the poor of those districts supplied.'

Thomas Bakewell had detected another prevarication in Loch's *Account* which he had not sufficient information himself to unravel. Stewart did so for him. Loch had suggested that the object of the improvements was to bestow on the people the profits of fishing, no less than to increase Patrick Sellar's sheep holdings and the rents of the Sutherland estate. He had described the allotments on the coast that were offered to all (of good character) who were removed from the interior. 'Reports are published', wrote Stewart, as though sparing the reader a personal introduction to Loch, 'of the unprecedented increase of the fisheries on the coast of the Highlands, proceeding, as it is said, from the late improvements; whereas it is well known that the increase is almost entirely occasioned by the resort of fishers from the south. . . . We may turn to an advertisement in the Inverness newspapers, describing sixty lots of land to be let in that country for fishing stations. To this notice is added a declaration that a *"decided preference will be given to strangers"*. Thus, while on the one hand the unfortunate natives are driven from their farms in the interior, a decided preference is given to strangers to settle on the coast.'

Such was the domestic background of the men whose military services in the Napoleonic war were the principal theme of Colonel Stewart's study.

They had brought extraordinary honour and profit to the family that had never even bothered to learn their language. 'In the year 1759 the Earl of Sutherland received proposals from Mr. Pitt to raise a Fencible regiment on his estate. The offer was readily accepted, and in nine days after his lordship arrived in Sutherland with his letters of service 1,100 men were assembled on the lawn before Dunrobin castle.' The regiment was disbanded after four years during which 'no restrictions had been required and no man had been punished'. Rob Donn Mackay, Strathnaver's great poet, had lamented the draining away of so many of the fittest young men of his country, but one of his own sons had shared the general enthusiasm for military service, and when he was killed in action it was Stewart of Garth who composed his epitaph.

In 1793 the Great Lady of Sutherland herself raised a regiment. 'When it was known in Sutherland that their Countess was expected to call forth a portion of the most able-bodied men on her extensive estates, the officers whom she appointed had only to make a selection of those who were best calculated to fill up the ranks of the regiment, which was completed in as short a time as the men could be collected from the rugged and distant districts they inhabited.' Nearly as many men were recruited also in those parts of Strathnaver still owned by the chief of Mackay and his relatives, and consequently distinguished at this time as the Reay country.

The regiment raised by the Countess was sent to Ireland, where it was remarked that 'the inhabitants were quiet, apparently less disaffected, and more regular in their habits', wherever this force speaking a kindred language was billeted. It was also noticed that 'while these soldiers indulged their naturally affectionate disposition by assisting their relatives by acts of liberality, they retained enough of money to enable them to pursue their social amusements: and it was a frequent practice to subscribe among themselves, and give dances to their acquaintances, not only in the barracks, but frequently in public rooms and places allotted for the purpose, which they hired. On these occasions the officers attended, as also many respectable inhabitants. . . . Among these men crimes which require severe punishments had no existence.' This Fencible regiment was disbanded in 1798, and two years later there came into being the 93rd regiment, or Sutherland Highlanders.[6]

A cairn beside the Naver river, in empty surroundings much overgrown with bracken, marks the spot where so many men flocked to join the Colours in the fertile strath so soon to be cleared of their families to make room for Sellar's sheep. 'There are few regiments', wrote Colonel Stewart, late of the Black Watch, 'in his Majesty's service which, in all those qualities requisite to constitute good soldiers, and valuable members of society, excel this respectable body of men. None of the Highland corps is superior to the 93rd regiment. I do not make comparisons in point of bravery, for if properly led they are all brave. But it is in those well regulated habits, of which so much has been already said, that the Sutherland Highlanders have for twenty years preserved an unvaried line of conduct. The light infantry company of this corps has been nineteen years without having a man punished. This single fact may be taken as sufficient evidence of good morals.'

Public recognition was sometimes given to the singular character of the Sutherland Highlanders. 'When punishments were to be inflicted on others, and the troops in camp, garrison or quarters assembled to witness their execution, the presence of the Sutherland Highlanders, either of the Fencibles or of the line, was often dispensed with, the effect of terror as a check to crime being in their case uncalled for, "as examples of that nature were not necessary for such honourable soldiers".'

Stewart also recalled an incident that occurred while the 93rd were stationed at the Cape of Good Hope. 'Being anxious to enjoy the advantages of religious instruction agreeably to the tenets of their national church, and there being no religious service in the garrison except the customary one of reading prayers to the soldiers on parade, the men of the 93rd regiment formed themselves into a congregation, appointed elders of their own number, engaged and paid a stipend (collected from the soldiers) to a clergyman of the Church of Scotland (who had gone out with an intention of teaching and preaching to the Caffres), and had Divine Service performed agreeably to the ritual of the established Church.'[7]

Such were the men whom Loch described as possessing 'habits and ideas quite incompatible with the customs of regular society and civilized life, adding greatly to those defects which characterize persons living in a loose and unformed state of society' (p. 24).

David Stewart's respect for his countrymen had been put to the sternest tests for many years, and when he considered the effrontery of the Lowland improvers in Sutherland he was no longer able to maintain his habitual restraint. 'Is it conceivable that the people at home should be so degraded, while their brothers and sons who become soldiers maintain an honourable character? The people ought not to be reproached with incapacity or immorality without better evidence than that of their prejudiced and unfeeling calumniators. If it be so, however, and if this virtuous and honourable race, which has contributed to raise and uphold the character of the British peasantry in the eyes of all Europe, are thus fallen, and so suddenly fallen; how great and powerful must be the cause, and how heavy the responsibility.'

There was, in Stewart's opinion, a particular form of deterioration in the Highlands which he was the first to connect with the policy of improvement. It was the steady decline in reputation of the ministers of the gospel amongst populations eminent for their piety. And since the removal of the Gaelic intelligentsia, the tacksmen and half-pay officers, these were sometimes the last remaining Gaels with a secure position and a higher education. These men had been appointed by the landlords since the reintroduction of patronage in the Church of Scotland, in direct contravention of the Treaty of Union.

The Rev. David Mackenzie, minister of the immense parish of Farr, was one of these men. The Sutherland estate had built him a manse resembling a mansion in 1814, surrounded by the best land in the district for his glebe. From it he had travelled to Inverness to give evidence at the trial of Patrick Sellar: in it he had signed or witheld his certificates of good character for his parishioners, the passports to those new allotments among the rocks that he could see from his windows. From the great pulpit that had been placed in his church in 1774 he translated and expounded the successive eviction orders to those who had sometimes walked as far as twenty miles to hear the Christian message. Stewart observed that such people were beginning to seek the Christian message from other lips, and it filled him with foreboding. That last great bulwark in which he so devoutly believed, the established Church, was becoming discredited amongst a people whose Christian faith was as strong as it had ever been.

'No religious order in modern times have been more useful and exemplary, by their instructions and practice, than the Scotch parochial clergy. Adding example to precept, they have taught the pure doctrines of Christianity in a manner clear and simple, and easily comprehended by their flock. Thus the religious tenets of the Highlanders, guided by their clergy, were blended with an impressive, captivating and, if I may be allowed to call it so, a salutary superstition, inculcating on the minds of all that an honourable and well spent life entailed a blessing on descendants, while a curse would descend on the successors of the wicked, the oppressor, and ungodly.' Such influences were on the wane, and 'the rude Highlanders are undergoing a process of civilization by new manners, new morals, and new religion, the progress of which is at once rapid and deplorable'.

Such was Stewart's bitter comment on the brash optimism of Loch; and before he had done he made a last appeal against the representations of such men. 'Can correct reports be expected from land agents and others, who are often ignorant of the country, the people and their language, and who often run over a district in one day, speaking to none except those appointed to meet them; and who, of course, will be careful to communicate anything but what is agreeable to their employers, more especially of the capabilities of the people, with whose ejection from their farms the first step of these agents commences?' He was burdened by the fear that his own book would prove too frail a weapon in defence of the reputation and safety of his race. 'I regret, for their sake, that the task to unveil the truth, to vindicate the injured, and by an honest and plain narrative of undoubted facts to point out the wrongs of the oppressed, has not fallen into abler hands; and that, among all the philanthropists whom this age has produced, none has stepped forward to advocate the cause of the calumniated Highlanders.'

But as it turned out, the person whom no one stepped forward to defend was the Countess-Marchioness of Sutherland and Stafford.

5

What the Swiss Said

1837

—◆•••◆—

THE man whose reluctance to defend the reputation of the
Great Lady of Sutherland appears, at this distance in time,
almost a personal affront was Sir Walter Scott. The greatest
Scotsman of his time had corresponded with Lady Stafford at
least since 1809, gratefully acknowledging the condescension of
her acquaintance, and flattering her in return with copies of his
compositions. On the other hand, Sir Walter also enjoyed the
acquaintance of Stewart of Garth. A lesser man might have
found himself in an awkward predicament in 1822, when
Stewart's book was published. He might have found it necessary
either to defend the reputation of a great lady against what he
considered to be a most injurious libel, or else to sever acquaintance with a great lady who had been unmasked as the source of
incalculable misery.

The Wizard of the North was reduced to neither of these
shifts. On the one hand he left to posterity his unequivocal
verdict: 'In too many instances the Highlands have been
drained not only of their superfluity of population, but of the
whole mass of the inhabitants dispossessed by an unrelenting
avarice which will one day be found to have been as shortsighted as it is unjust and selfish.' On the other hand he contrived
to remain as ever 'dear Lady marchioness, your truly obliged
and grateful humble servant', particularly when in 1825 he
solicited her interest over the appointment of his son-in-law
Lockhart as Sheriff of Sutherland. But Scott reverenced a

marchioness at all times, and perhaps in any circumstances, while his real feelings for the Highlanders about whom he wrote such popular romances can be glimpsed from this comment to Lady Stafford on Marshal Macdonald's proposed visit to South Uist. 'I have a notion the place is horribly desolate, without grandeur of any kind, even that of sterility. I question whether it will be improved by a parcel of poor smoke-dried relatives who will rush on him to get what they can.' The Marshal was another matter: he had been created by Napoleon Duke of Tarentum, and if there was anyone Scott reverenced more than a marchioness, it was a duke.

If the attitude of Sir Walter Scott to the issue of the clearances is devious yet clear, so too is that of the Great Lady of Sutherland. For the attacks that had been made on the administration of her estates were ignored, and the policy that had been so bitterly criticized was continued and expanded. The house of Sutherland-Stafford was shown to be beyond the reach of vulgar clamour, and its agent was given a position in which he shared a little of its immunity. In 1827, two years after Stewart's third edition was published, and the year in which he became a major-general, James Loch was given a seat in Parliament representing a Cornish constituency.

Meanwhile advantage was taken of the improvidence of the chief of Mackay, Eric, seventh Lord Reay. Loans were made to him by the Staffords, upon the security of the 400,000 Scottish acres of Strathnaver that still remained in his possession. He would not or could not meet these debts, and in 1829 sold his entire property to the Staffords for £300,000. In the following year Mackay of Bighouse sold Strath Halladale, the last remaining portion of Strathnaver owned by a Mackay, to the same family. The ancient dream of the Gordon earls had been realized at last through the wealth of the Leveson-Gowers, and the administration of James Loch: and in 1830 Loch received appropriate recognition when he was returned unopposed as M.P. for the Northern Burghs.[8]

General Stewart of Garth perhaps did not hear of these latest developments, for in 1829 he was appointed Governor of St. Lucia in the West Indies, where he died of fever.

The jubilation with which Patrick Sellar learned of the latest purchases may be assessed from the difficulty he had experienced in persuading Lord Reay to extend the eviction policy in the lands adjacent to his own. 'My Lord, some time ago your Lordship's brother wrote me that Mr. Forbes had not removed one of his subtenants, whom as dependents and servants he keeps doing mischief and ploughing in the winter land of Ben Hope—a thing which in the face of his written promise to your Lordship I thought very surprising. I saw Mr. Forbes soon after, and was assured by him they should all quit along with himself at Whitsunday 1820 and leave the land unploughed. But to my great surprise I received a letter from him again on the 16th April in quite a different strain, maintaining that he would plough and keep under-tenants as he pleased. Now my Lord, that no misunderstanding may possibly arise between your Lordship and me by silence, as was the case with Mr. Houston, I give your Lordship timely notice of all this to intimate that if the *banditti* presently kept on Ben Hope farm are to have possession until Whitsunday 1821, on the pretext that they have ploughed 1820 and must consume their straw . . . then I cannot enter into possession at Whitsunday 1820 as was intended.' The tables were turned now on the Gaelic *banditti* who tried to upset Sellar's Whitsunday celebrations.

And now at last it appeared that Lord Pitmilly's words, uttered fourteen years before in the court-room at Inverness, had come true. The case against the Sutherland improvements had been made available to all who could read the English language and had been met with indifference. High above the clamour the Great Lady of Sutherland remained unshaken in her purposes, and now there was no dark corner left in all Strathnaver where the smoke-dried *banditti* might hide from the awful chastisement of her benevolence. A new map was prepared in which the region itself vanished into a Sutherland, large enough for a dukedom.

So it proved when in 1833 the Marquess of Stafford was created first Duke of Sutherland: and it is sad to contemplate that he lived only six months in the enjoyment of an honour for which he paid so heavily in money and in reputation. But for a longer period he had enjoyed a different honour. His character had been defended by a native of Staffordshire who was not his dependant, and without solicitation.

In his death the first Duke of Sutherland was also spared a

most wounding blow to the honour of his house, leaving the Countess-Duchess to bear it alone. The policy of the Sutherland clearances was raised in the most influential medium of European thought, the French language, by Simonde de Sismondi, the most respected social scientist of his age.

Sismondi was a Swiss scholar of independent fortune whose massive contributions to European thought had earned him recognition in the centres of learning of Germany, France and Switzerland, Italy and Russia. He engaged in a series of studies on political economy as part of an even larger thesis, and one of these studies he devoted exclusively to the present predicament of the Scottish Gaelic peoples. He related his remarks, of course, to his main thesis; but it was on grounds of humanity and in defence of civilized standards of conduct that he made the first direct attack upon the personal character of the Countess-Duchess of Sutherland which she had ever had to face. And he made it in the form of an appeal to the civilized people of Europe, in the name of that civilization and in its language, against behaviour 'as shameful as it was criminal'.

He apologized to his readers that he must burden them with so distasteful a theme. 'There is something so absurd and revolting in interpreting as a form of progress the destruction of the happiness, of the liberty, of the very existence of a race, in the interests of wealth.' This fate had befallen 'the Gaelic race, descendants of the ancient Celts, reduced today to 340,000 in number': the lands they had cultivated generation after generation had been 'handed over to foreign shepherds, their houses and villages have been torn down or destroyed by fire, and the evicted members of this mountain race were left no choice but either to erect huts by the sea-shore and try to preserve their miserable existence by fishing, or to cross this sea and seek their fortune in the wastes of America'.

It was not always easy to arrive at the truth of what occurred in these semi-military operations that they called 'the clearing of an estate', but happily a certain James Loch had published a full account in 1820 of the most notorious that had taken place.

The size of the territory involved Sismondi explained by saying that it was larger than the *Departement* of the Haut-Rhin in France. This land contained 15,000 inhabitants at the time 'when the Countess of Sutherland inherited her domains and brought them as her dowry to the Marquess of Stafford'.

But Sismondi had satisfied himself that the Countess-Duchess retained control of all that was done in her country, and he went even further than Bakewell had done in dismissing her shy and retiring husband from any responsibility. 'The Duchess of Sutherland is, beyond question, an extremely clever woman; she administers her immense fortune with intelligence; she augments it, and for it she prepares fresh enterprises in the future.' Unlike all previous authors, Sismondi attributed the responsibility for everything that had occurred in Sutherland to her alone, and he was careful not to mention the late Duke again.[9]

The Countess required that her country should contribute the utmost to maintain her station 'amidst the extravagance and wealth of London'. The young men of her estate could no longer assist by offering their lives in her family regiment, for this form of export trade had now declined. The export of whisky, whose distillation in the area Sismondi noted, had not yet been thought of; and it was rigorously suppressed on the estate. The clever Countess decided to invest in sheep and 'between the year 1811 and the year 1820 these 15,000 inhabitants, consisting of about three thousand families, were hunted, or in Mr. Loch's gentler phrase "removed" from the whole interior of the county, under his supervision. All their villages were demolished or burnt, and all their fields converted into pasture.'

It was some time, Sismondi observed, before these events attracted much attention in the English-speaking parts of Britain, 'since this revolution took place eight hundred miles from London, in a semi-barbarous country whose language is incomprehensible throughout the rest of the empire'. But as rumours of atrocities began to trickle south, 'attention began to focus particularly on the Marchioness of Stafford, heir to the earldom of Sutherland'. So far Sismondi had done scarcely more than to condense Loch's own account, and he went little farther when he said, 'the Marchioness of Stafford believed she did not deserve the severe judgment that people were beginning to pass on her, and it was with the object of justifying herself before the tribunal of public opinion that the book was composed in which we find these details'.

Its author had set out to prove 'not only that the Marchioness of Stafford has used her rights solely within limits permitted her today by law, but in addition that in exercising them she has never overlooked the preservation of the lives of her vassals, for whom she believed herself responsible'.

Sismondi suggested that civilized people might be expected to look farther than this. 'As for us, what we believe to be worthy of study in this book has nothing to do with evidence of the conduct of a great lady, however intelligent or generous: it is the essential quality of a system of law that has abolished the ancient sanctions of property established by custom; it is the application of the principle that the proprietor is the best judge of his own interest and that of the people in what concerns their property.'

The generosity of the Countess-Marchioness-Duchess was indeed rather odd as Loch described it. 'Mr. Loch meanwhile insists that the Marchioness of Stafford has shown a great deal more humanity than any of her neighbours. She has concerned herself over the lot of those she has removed. She has offered them asylum in her own country, and while she has taken back from them 794,000 acres of land which they had possessed from time immemorial, she has generously left them about 6,000 of these, that is, two acres per family. These 6,000 acres available for use as a refuge for the small tenants were formerly waste, and yielded nothing to the proprietor. All the same, she has not made a gift of them. She has assessed them at an average rent of two shillings and sixpence per acre, and no leases have been granted for longer than seven years.'

This extraordinary concern for petty profit, which Loch had concealed behind the mask of philanthropy, received more succinct comment from Sismondi than from the farmer or soldier who had preceded him. 'We may not doubt for an instant that the destruction of the ownership, the customs, the loyalties, the whole existence of a little race of people has prodigiously increased the already colossal fortune of the Countess of Sutherland. But Mr. Loch is concerned to show that it has also increased the wealth of the country.' He speaks of roads and bridges, but what Sismondi would like to know is the fate of a particular group of people whom Loch mentioned 'as having abandoned the mountains of Kildonan and the valleys of the

Naver and the Helmsdale rivers, and as having left the country altogether: and the author does not inform us what became of them'.

Like Bakewell and Stewart of Garth before him, Sismondi could not resist easing apart the cracks in the fabric of James Loch's argument. And between the three of them, a Gael, an Englishman and a Swiss of widely differing pursuits, they left few undiscovered absurdities for the detection of future readers. Indeed, it is very astonishing that James Loch, who was qualified in the law both of Scotland and England, could have contrived a piece of advocacy so incompetent, or that the Countess-Duchess could have been so wanting in judgement as to suppose that it would help, rather than injure, her reputation. For unless some member of her estate should ever combine sufficient courage and knowledge of the English language to write a book, Loch's account of what had occurred would remain a unique mine of information, while his arguments would continue to make sport for anyone of the least intellectual capacity.

But Sismondi was concerned with something more serious than sport. He was concerned for the future of what remained of the Celtic race in Scotland. He thought of those people of the glens seeking to raise a few crops in their wretched allotments on the coast and learning the harsh rules of seamanship in the dangerous northern seas. What security had this remnant of the evicted race? 'In seven years, in fourteen years, at each expiration of their lease, these families of Sutherland, already deprived of their homeland, will be exposed anew to the errors, the false calculations, the dissipation, avarice, folly or injustice of the proprietor, who without the slightest responsibility will hold their fate in his or her hands.'

Even if the proprietor had been a person of reputable conduct, and one capable of choosing respectable servants, the law of the country remained a disgrace to Europe. 'If the Marchioness of Stafford was indeed entitled by law to replace the population of an entire province by twenty-nine families of foreigners and some hundreds of thousands of sheep, they should hurry up and abolish such an odious law, both in respect of her and of all the others in her position.'

Thomas Bakewell had considered legislation, and dismissed the idea as impracticable. It was perhaps a little less impracticable when Sismondi wrote in 1837, because the Reform Act had at least paved a way to a shift of power in the Parliament of landowners. But it might take another fifty years before that power could be touched in the far north, whose representatives in Parliament were the Duke of Sutherland in the House of Lords, and James Loch in the House of Commons. To Sismondi, who saw the British law as a barbarous relic long ago abolished in civilized European countries, it was not conceivable that the law remained at all, except by an unfortunate oversight that the intelligent and generous British people would be most anxious to correct.

'Legislation has not ceased during eight centuries, in the whole continent of Europe, to guarantee and improve the lot of the feuee, the vassal, the serf who depended on a lord; to assert the independence of the peasant, to protect him with the armour of prescriptive right, to turn customary into legal rights, to place him beyond the reach of the exactions of his lord. . . . The law has given the Swiss peasant the guarantee of perpetual ownership, while in the British empire it has given this same guarantee to the Scottish lord, and left the peasant in insecurity. Let anyone compare the two countries and judge the two systems.'

Sismondi allowed his mind to dwell on the possible results of extending the British law to his own country, 'which resembles Scotland in its lakes and mountains, in its climate which so often confounds the hope of the labourer, in the character, manners and customs of its children, and which was also divided at this time among a small number of noblemen. If the earls of Kyburg and Lentzburg, of Hapsburg and Gruyeres had been protected by British laws, they would find themselves today in exactly the position in which the earls of Sutherland were twenty years ago. Some of their number might perhaps have developed the same taste for improvements, and several Swiss republics would have been driven from the Alps to make way for flocks of sheep.'

And yet it would scarcely have been possible. For 'before reaching such a barbarous resolution it had been necessary for the nobleman to cease utterly to share the views, attachments and sense of decency of his fellow men. It had been necessary not merely for him to believe himself no longer their father or their brother, but even to have ceased to believe himself of the same race. It had been necessary for an ignoble greed to extinguish in him the sense of consanguinity to which their ancestors had trusted when they had bequeathed the destiny of their people to his good faith.' Sismondi, who had moved much among the great in Europe, had not encountered anyone he believed capable of behaving like the Countess-Marchioness-Duchess.

Such was the verdict added in the French language to those that had been published already in England, and the seventy-two-year-old Duchess of Sutherland, whose husband had once been British ambassador in Paris, must have been very angry indeed. She had good reason to be. For centuries her family had been the most loyal supporters in the north of Edinburgh's ancient aim, the destruction of the Celtic people of Scotland, the obliteration of their culture and language. She had brought this great objective within sight of realization throughout the immense area of Sutherland and Strathnaver, and in doing so she had exposed her reputation to the attacks of Highlander, Englishman, and European. Yet the only one of all her Lowland Scottish compatriots who had stepped forward to vindicate her name in the literary arena was one whom she paid for his services, and he appeared to have done it with remarkably little skill.

But perhaps it was he who composed the fulsome address signed by over a thousand of her well-disciplined tenants, and perhaps she was able to turn to this document for consolation. It was indeed a most eloquent testimony in her favour. Posterity would never know what her tenantry said about her in their own barbaric tongue: the tongue and all it had ever said would soon be but a dying echo among empty hills. But the address with all its signatures would be preserved among the Dunrobin muniments till the end of time. The Duchess, who had already suffered so much, was at least left with this comfort.

She died in 1839, by which time one of her former tenants had learned English rather better than Loch could have wished, in fact with the precocity of a thoroughly bad character. And instead of disappearing altogether when he was removed from the estate, as a destitute stone-mason ought to have done, he actually turned to publishing his exciting adventures in instalments, in the English language. People could read the enthralling story of a battle for a certificate of good character, of the midwinter adventures of homeless children, of Patrick Sellar's Whitsunday fire festivals. Nothing so entertaining as this had appeared in all the varied literature of the Duchess of Sutherland's long career. It was the translation of all the Gaelic poems and stories that the English speaker could not understand; it was the voice of over a thousand tenants who had put their signatures to an English address; it was the epitaph for the tomb of the Great Lady of Sutherland.

6

What the Stone-Mason Said
1841

————◆◆◆◆◆————

O N the summit of Ben Bhraggie, already such a conspicuous landmark above the castle of Dunrobin, a huge statue of the Duke of Sutherland was erected by order of his widow and her factor. The thoughtful and retiring Duke gazes in effigy over the country he occasionally visited during his life, and whose name he adopted for six short months. But Donald Macleod the stone-mason has no memorial except a place in the hearts of every one of his countrymen in all parts of the world. His birthplace and all its surrounding townships have been eradicated as completely as if Timur the Terrible had passed that way in anger, and it is not easy to locate the spot hallowed by so much gratitude and esteem.

The modern road that passes down the unpopulated valley of the Naver divides at the lodge of Syre. One branch of it travels through empty wastes to the almost uninhabited valley of Kildonan, the other continues beside the Naver river to its loch. No human landmark any longer recalls the vanished village of Rossal whose ruins were still visible to Sellar as he travelled that way on his journeys south.

Donald Macleod was born at Rossal. His father was a small-holder, but he appears to have been a mason also, for Donald recorded: 'I served an apprenticeship in the mason trade to my father.' That was at the time when their neighbour William Chisholm was evicted, and Donald recalled this incident of his youth. 'I was present at the pulling down and burning of the house of William Chisholm, Badinloskin, in which was lying his wife's mother, an old bed-ridden woman of nearly 100 years of age, none of the family being present.'

It is a new dimension to the story that young Donald alone had been present to restrain the fire-raisers when they first reached the house. 'I informed the persons about to set fire to the house of this circumstance, and prevailed on them to wait till Mr. Sellar came. On his arrival I told him of the poor old woman being in a condition unfit for removal. He replied, "Damn her, the old witch, she has lived too long; let her burn." Fire was immediately set to the house, and the blankets in which she was carried were in flames before she could be got out. She was placed in a little shed, and it was with great difficulty they were prevented from firing it also. The old woman's daughter arrived while the house was on fire, and assisted the neighbours in removing her mother out of the flames and smoke, presenting a picture of horror which I shall never forget, but cannot attempt to describe. She died within five days.'[10]

Donald explained how it was that he could already enjoy the privilege of the new factor's English conversation. 'For some years I followed the practice of going south during the summer months for the purpose of improving in my trade and obtaining better wages, and returning in the winter to enjoy the society of my family and friends; and also, to my grief, to witness the scenes of devastation that were going on.'

In 1818 Donald married a native of Farr parish, and this was the cause of his abandoning his visits to the south. For two years later his father-in-law died soon after being evicted, 'leaving six orphans in a state of entire destitution to be provided for; for he had lost his all, in common with the other ejected inhabitants of the country. This helpless family now fell to my care, and in order to discharge my duty to them more effectually I wished to give up my summer excursions, and settle and pursue my business at home.'

At this time the population had been driven to the north coast, often in successive removals of people who had just built homes on new allotments and dug ground that had never been worked before. Loch himself had instanced those of Dunviden for their cheerful co-operation. 'Mr. Sellar', Donald Macleod noted, 'had three large farms, one of which was twenty-five miles long; and in some places nine or ten miles broad, situated in the barony of Strathnaver.'

Loch had already explained in his book the benefits of the coastal allotments. Donald Macleod used a different emphasis. The object of the policy, he said, was 'to force those who could not or would not leave the country to draw their subsistence from the sea by fishing; and in order to deprive them of any other means, the lots were not only made small (varying from one to three acres), but their nature and situation rendered them unfit for any useful purpose. . . . The spots allowed them could not be called land, being composed of narrow strips, promontories, cliffs and precipices, rocks and deep crevices, interspersed with bogs and morasses. The whole quite useless to the superiors.'

Bakewell, Stewart, and Sismondi had all drawn particular attention to Loch's passage about the generosity of the Countess in providing these coastal allotments for her people. Donald Macleod's description of them was so directly at variance with Loch's that anyone could now see one of the two men was not telling the truth. And anyone can still see, by inspecting those sites today, whether it was the stone-mason of Strathnaver or the Member of Parliament from Edinburgh.

Loch had written of the need to force the ignorant and un-co-operative natives to the coast as rapidly as possible in their own best interests, and he had mentioned the disastrous winter of 1816–17, during which disease and starvation had been relieved only by the generosity of the Staffords. Donald Macleod also described the havoc that was consummated at the coastal allotments. Of the winter Loch mentioned, he recorded that it 'commenced by the snow falling in large quantities in the month of October, and continued with increased rigour so that the difficulty—almost impossibility—of the people, without barns or shelter of any kind, securing their crops may be easily conceived. I have seen scores of the poor outcasts employed for weeks together, with the snow from two to four feet deep, watching the corn from being devoured by the now hungry sheep of the incoming tenants; carrying on their backs—horses being unavailable in such a case—across the country without roads, on an average of twenty miles to their new allotments on the sea coast, any portion of their grain and potatoes they could secure under such dreadful circumstances. . . . They had to subsist entirely on potatoes dug out of the snow; cooking them as they could in the open air, among the ruins of their once comfortable dwellings.'

Loch had stated that relief to the amount of £12,000 was sent to the country, besides medicine (p. 21). 'I look upon it to be a fabrication,' Macleod wrote, 'or if the money really was sent by the noble proprietors, it must have been retained by those entrusted with its distribution; for to my knowledge it never came to the hands of any of the small tenants. There was indeed a considerable quantity of meal sent, though far from enough to afford effectual relief, but this meal represented to be given in charity was charged at the following Martinmas term, at the rate of 50 shillings per boll. Payment was rigorously exacted, and those who had cattle were obliged to give them up for that purpose.' This was what Bakewell had suspected.

But one part of Loch's statement was confirmed by Macleod. 'There was a considerable quantity of medicine given to the ministers for distribution for which no charge was made, and this was the whole amount of relief afforded.'

Loch had explained in meticulous detail why it had been decided to accelerate and complete the removals during the years 1819–20. Donald Macleod attempted to describe what he witnessed of this process. 'Strong parties for each district, furnished with faggots and other combustibles, rushed on the dwellings of this devoted people and immediately commenced setting fire to them, proceeding in their work with the greatest rapidity till about three hundred houses were in flames. The consternation and confusion were extreme; little or no time were given for removal of persons or property—the people striving to remove the sick and the helpless before the fire should reach them—next, struggling to save the most valuable of their effects. The cries of the women and children—the roaring of the affrighted cattle hunted at the same time by the yelling dogs of the shepherds amid the smoke and fire—altogether presented a scene that completely baffles description.

'A dense cloud of smoke enveloped the whole country by day, and even extended far on the sea; at night an awfully grand, but terrific scene presented itself—all the houses in an extensive district in flames at once. I myself ascended a height about eleven o'clock in the evening and counted two hundred and fifty blazing houses, many of the owners of which were my relations, and all of whom I personally knew; but whose present condition, whether in or out of the flames, I could not tell. The conflagration lasted six days.'

Some of the people tried to escape forthwith from the lands of the Countess-Marchioness. 'While the burning was going on, a small sloop arrived, laden with quick lime, and when discharging her cargo the skipper agreed to take as many of the people to Caithness as he could carry.' This vessel must have unloaded its cargo at the mouth of the Naver river, where the salmon station is still to be seen. 'About twenty families went on board, filling the deck, hold and every part of the vessel. There were childhood and age, male and female, sick and well, with a small portion of their effects saved from the flames, all huddled together in heaps. Many of these persons had never been on sea before, and when they began to sicken a scene indescribable ensued. To add to their miseries, a storm and contrary winds prevailed, so that instead of a day or two, the usual time of passage, it was nine days before they reached Caithness.'

One of these families was particularly fortunate to reach the sloop in time. 'Robert Mackay, whose whole family were in a fever or otherwise ailing, had to carry his two daughters on his back, a distance of about twenty miles. He accomplished this by first carrying one, and laying her down in the open air, and returning, did the same with the other, till he reached the seashore and then went with them on board the lime vessel.'

Others were less fortunate, particularly the aged and sick. 'An old man of the same name betook himself to a deserted mill, and lay there unable to move; and to the best of my recollection he died there. He had no sustenance but what he obtained by licking the dust and refuse of the meal strewed about, and was defended from the rats and other vermin by his faithful collie.' One woman developed a peculiar form of insanity; 'whenever she saw a stranger she cried out, with a terrific tone and manner, "O sin Sellar!" (Oh, there's Sellar!)' Donald Macleod recorded the fate of a large number of individuals in this way, as they recurred to his mind twenty years later.

The coastal allotments upon which the residue settled

extended from Bettyhill by the mouth of the Naver river east-
wards past the villages of Swordly, Kirtomy, Armadale, and
Strathy. There is no safe harbourage along the whole of this
deeply indented, rocky and storm-swept coast; but here men
who had never learned seamanship were compelled by hunger
to seek their food in the sea. Here, as Sismondi had noticed, the
Countess-Duchess succeeded in raising rents from the ocean
where the land she leased was not worth a rent.

'Numerous as were the casualties, and of almost daily
occurrence, yet the escapes, many of them extraordinary, were
happily still more frequent.' Donald Macleod preserved several
instances. 'William Mackay, a respectable man, shortly after
settling in his allotment on the coast, went one day to explore
his new possession: and in venturing to examine more nearly
the ware growing within the flood mark, was suddenly swept
away by a splash of the sea from one of the adjoining creeks, and
lost his life before the eyes of his miserable wife, in the last
month of her pregnancy, and three helpless children who were
left to deplore his fate. James Campbell, a man also with a
family, on attempting to catch a peculiar kind of small fish among
the rocks, was carried away by the sea and never seen afterwards. Bell Mackay, a married woman and mother of a family
while in the act of taking up salt water to make salt of, was
carried away in a similar manner, and nothing more seen of her.
Robert Mackay, who with his family were suffering extreme
want, in endeavouring to procure some sea-fowls' eggs among
the rocks, lost his hold; and falling from a prodigious height
was dashed to pieces, leaving a wife and five destitute children
behind him. John Macdonald, while fishing, was swept off the
rocks and never seen more.'

But as Macleod had said, there were also times when good
luck compensated their inexperience. 'One instance of this kind,
in which I bore a part myself, I will here relate. Five venturous
young men, of whom I was one, having bought an old crazy
boat that had long been laid up as useless, and having procured
lines of an inferior description for haddock fishing, put to sea
without sail, helm or compass, with three patched oars; only
one of the party ever having been on sea before. This apparently
insane attempt gathered a crowd of spectators. . . . We boldly
ventured on, human life having become reduced in value, and after

a night spent on the sea, in which we freshmen suffered severely from sea-sickness, to the great astonishment of the people on shore, the *Heather-Boat*, as she was called, reached the land in the morning—all hands safe, with a very good take of fishes.'

What is the explanation for Donald Macleod's adventures on the sea as part owner of the crazy old *Heather-Boat*? He was one of the few inhabitants who possessed a ready-made escape route from this land of fire, disease, and starvation. He was a stone-mason who had earned his living in the Lowlands for many years, only returning in the winter to his family. He wrote that the death of his father-in-law during the great removals kept him at home to look after his wife's family; and no doubt there was plenty of work for a trained mason among the new allotments, even if there was little or nothing to pay him with. Perhaps Donald stayed on simply to contribute his professional skill in his people's dire need, and to give his family the comfort of his presence.

But it seems probable that he had already apprehended a more important reason for remaining in his country than these, when he could so easily have escaped. Someone must turn and face the forces that were destroying his people, test the legality of each one of their actions, and dispute every inch of the ground before retreating. It was the martyr's role, and Donald Macleod was the man who adopted it. He faced the entire armament of the Sutherland estate with what weapons he possessed, his knowledge of English, his independent trade, his intelligence, and a courage that never yielded. He suffered a martyr's fate as he probably knew he would, but he achieved an object that remained for a native of the area to win, now that the protests of Stewart and Sismondi had proved ineffectual.

Donald Macleod was strengthened by the fact that he did not fit into the categories of malicious and credulous persons, against whose opinions Loch had warned the readers of his *Account*. He had not been a tacksman or half-pay officer, and he was manifestly unlike Loch's description of the indolent peasant ignorant of English. How soon he attracted the attention of the establishment as a turbulent and dangerous character is not easy to determine, until the first steps were taken to get rid of him. But it is clear that the method adopted was to deprive him of his livelihood, and it may be on this account that he joined the venture of the *Heather-Boat*. He did mention that preference was given to strangers in such public works as might have given him a livelihood in the district, and that he soon became a marked man.

He described the first dangerous assault on him as having taken place in 1827. 'It was in this year that her Ladyship, the proprietrix, and suite made a visit to Dunrobin castle. Previous to her arrival the clergy and factors, and the new tenants, set about raising a subscription throughout the country to provide a costly set of ornaments, with complimentary inscriptions, to be presented to her ladyship in name of her tenantry. Emissaries were dispatched for this purpose even to the small tenantry, located on the moors and barren cliffs, and every means used to wheedle or scare them into contributing. They were told that those who would subscribe would thereby secure her ladyship's and the factor's favour, and those who could not or would not were given to understand, very significantly, what they had to expect.' Macleod did not mention whether Strathnaver also provided any of the thousand signatures that accompanied the gift and the address.

While this ceremony took place at Dunrobin, one of a very different kind was enacted in Strathnaver.

'If any chose to say I owed them money, they had no more to do than summon me to court, in which the factor was judge. A decreet, right or wrong, was sure to issue.' Macleod described how this machinery of justice was adapted for his downfall. 'In the year 1827 I was summoned for £5–8s, which I had previously paid. In this case the factor was both pursuer and judge. I defended, and produced receipts and other vouchers of payment having been made. All went for nothing. The factor, pursuer and judge commenced the following dialogue:

' "Well Donald, do you owe this money?"

' "I would like to see the pursuer before I would enter into any defences."

' "I'll pursue you."

' "I thought you were my judge, Sir."

' "I'll both pursue and judge you. Did you not promise me on a former occasion that you would pay this debt?"

' "No, Sir."

' "John Mackay (constable), seize the defender."

'I was accordingly collared like a criminal and kept a prisoner in an adjoining room for some hours, and afterwards placed again at the bar, when the conversation continued.

' "Well Donald, what have you got to say now? Will you pay the money?"

' "Just the same, Sir, as before you imprisoned me. I deny the debt."

' "Well Donald, you are one of the damnedest rascals in existence, but if you have the sum pursued for between heaven and hell, I'll make you pay it, whatever receipts you may hold, and I'll get you removed from the estate."

' "Mind, Sir, you are in a magisterial capacity."

' "I'll let you know that." '

Donald Macleod sent a personal petition to Lord and Lady Stafford. 'In consequence of this, on the very term day on which I had been ordered to remove I received a verbal message from one of the under-factors, that it was the noble proprietor's pleasure that I should retain possession, repair my houses and provide my fuel as usual, until Mr. Loch should come to Sutherlandshire, and then my case would be investigated.'

It is curious that Donald did not mention the name of the factor, pursuer, and judge, unless he expected his readers to recognize the voice of the late factor, Patrick Sellar. But whoever was his opponent, Donald spent his respite in preparing for the trial of strength, and for this his first and indispensable requirement was a certificate of good character from the minister. 'I waited on my parish minister, the Rev. Mr. Mackenzie, requesting him to give me a certificate; and then, after him, I could obtain the signatures of the elders and as many of the other parishioners as might be necessary. He made no objection at the time, but alleging he was then engaged, said I could send my wife for it. I left directions with her accordingly and returned to my work. The same night the factor, my pretended creditor and judge, had the minister and his family to spend the evening with him.'

The timing of this invitation indicates that the minister may have made a journey of just over a mile from his grand new manse to the ferry at Invernaver, then another of about the same distance to the new farm-house which still stands at *Achaidh nam Buairidhean*, the Field of Bellowing.

'In the morning a messenger was dispatched from his reverence to my wife, to say that she need not take the trouble of calling for the certificate, as he had changed his mind. Some days after I returned and waited on the Rev. gentleman to inquire the cause of this change. I had great difficulty in obtaining an audience, and when at last I did, it was little to my satisfaction. His manner was contemptuous and forbidding. At last he told me that he could not give me a certificate as I was at variance with the factor, that my conduct was unscriptural, as I obeyed not those set in authority over me.'

This occurred in June 1830, and Macleod had heard that Loch was due in September. He continued to pester the minister and 'many of his elders and parishioners pleaded and remonstrated with him on my behalf, well knowing that little attention would be paid in high quarters to my complaints, however just, without his sanction; and considerable excitement prevailed in the parish about this dispute. But the minister remained immoveable.'

In the end Donald Macleod took even less scriptural action. 'I then got a certificate prepared myself, and readily obtained the signatures of the elders and neighbouring parishioners to the amount of several hundreds.' And this revealed how dangerous is the infection of courage; for the signatures on Macleod's testimonial were not likely to earn the same favour as those on the address to Lady Stafford, especially when 'presented to Mr. Loch, along with the before-mentioned memorial'.

Loch looked over the certificate mentioned above, with the three or four sheets full of names attached to it. He looked at it for some time, perhaps surprised at the number of signatures, and then said:

' "I cannot see the minister's name here. How is this?"

' "I applied to the minister and he would not sign it."

' "Why?"

' "He stated as his reason that I was at variance with the factors." '

One of the factors who was present with the pair interjected, "That is a falsehood", but Loch himself continued:

' "I will wait upon Mr. Mackenzie on the subject."

' "Will you allow me, Sir, to meet you and Mr. Mackenzie face to face when he is asked to give his reasons?"

' "Why will you not believe what he says?"

' "I have got too much reason to doubt it; but if he attempts to deny what I have stated, I hope you will allow him to be examined on oath."

' "By no means. We must surely believe the minister." '

Macleod said that Loch dismissed him in apparent good humour, but in fact his fate was sealed, and nothing could have contributed more to this than the number of signatures, revealing the extent of Donald's popularity.

The authorities were compelled to take special precautions in dealing with a man so impervious to intimidation, and so liable to arouse widespread disaffection in the district. They guarded themselves against the second danger by the use of surprise, and they overcame the first by concentrating on the only weak link in Donald Macleod's armour—the presence of his wife and family on the Sutherland estate.

These lived at Armadale, nearly eight miles east along the coast from the manse of Farr. The estate of Armadale had been purchased from a Mackay and was let to William Innes of Sandside in Caithness. Its mansion house (or Bighouse, as these are often called in the neighbourhood) and farm buildings still stand either side of the main coast road. The village extends along the headland to the fishing station which may have witnessed the adventures of the *Heather-Boat*. Here, on the 20th October 1830, about a month after Loch's investigation, Donald Macleod's wife was raided without warning.

'At this time', her husband recorded, 'I was working in Wick, and on that night had laboured under such great uneasiness and apprehension of something wrong at home that I could get no rest, and at last determined to set out and see how it fared with my family.' It fared ill, as he soon discovered. 'On that day a messenger with a party of eight men following entered my dwelling (I being away about forty miles off at work), about 3 o'clock, just as the family were rising from dinner. My wife was seized with a fearful panic at seeing the fulfilment of all her worst forebodings about to take place. The party allowed no time for parley, but having put out the family with violence, proceeded to fling out the furniture, bedding and other effects in quick time, and after extinguishing the fire, proceeded to nail up the doors and windows in the face of the helpless woman, with a sucking infant at her breast and three other children, the eldest under eight years of age, at her side.'

The people of the district were warned against offering shelter to Donald Macleod's family; and they may be forgiven for recognizing how pointless it would have been to extend God's judgement on unscriptural behaviour any further.[11] 'Wind, rain and sleet were ushering in a night of extraordinary darkness and violence, even in that inclement region. . . . After spending most part of the night in fruitless attempts to obtain the shelter of a roof or hovel, my wife at last returned to collect some of her scattered furniture, and erect with her own hands a temporary shelter against the walls of her late comfortable residence.' Only those acquainted with the wind force of the north coast of Scotland in these conditions will fully understand Donald's remark: 'The wind dispersed her materials as fast as she could collect them.'

Donald's wife now made a most enterprising decision, especially remarkable in a mother. 'Buckling up her children, including the one she had hitherto held at her breast, in the best manner she could, she left them in charge of the eldest (now a soldier in the 78th regiment), giving them such victuals as she could collect, and prepared to take the road for Caithness, fifteen miles off, in such a night and by such a road as might have appalled a stout heart of the other sex.' She was travelling towards her husband, and into lands beyond the power of Loch.

'She had not proceeded many miles when she met with a good Samaritan and acquaintance of the name of Donald Macdonald, who, disregarding the danger he incurred, opened his door to her, refreshed and consoled her, and still under cover of night, accompanied her to the dwelling of William Innes Esq of Sandside.' The nights are long on the north coast at this time of year.

Sandside is a large estate by the village of Reay in Caithness, hardly ten miles from Thurso. Its proprietor was not merely tenant of Armadale: he must also have harboured a detestation for the rulers of Sutherland that overrode his sense of loyalty to the landowning class to which he belonged. Through this remarkable circumstance, the stratagem to rid the country of Donald Macleod was frustrated. Innes of Sandside offered his family accommodation on the property at Armadale protected by his lease; and Donald himself reached Sandside on his journey west while his wife was still resting there. 'After a brief recital of the events of the previous night, she implored me to leave her and seek the children, of whose fate she was ignorant.'

The fate of the children was no less extraordinary than the premonition that had driven their father from Wick the previous night, or the instant succour of Innes of Sandside. The eldest boy, who was seven years old, had decided to make an expedition of his own. 'He took the infant on his back, and the other two took hold of him by the kilt, and in this way they travelled in darkness, through rough and smooth, bog and mire, till they arrived at a great-aunt's house; when, finding the door open they bolted in, and the boy advancing to his astonished aunt, laid his infant burden in her lap without saying a word, and proceeding to unbuckle the other two, he placed them before the fire without waiting for invitation. The goodman here rose, and said he must leave the house and seek a lodging for himself, as he could not think of turning the children out, and yet dreaded the ruin threatened to any that would harbour or shelter them. And he had no doubt his house would be watched to see if he should transgress against the order. His wife, a pious woman, upbraided him with cowardice, and declared that if there was a legion of devils watching her she would not put out the children or leave the house either. So they got leave to remain till I found them next day: but the man, impelled by his fears, did go and obtain a lodging two miles off.'

Only one serious problem remained when they were installed in their new home. The long process of peat-cutting was completed, and they had lost their whole winter supply with the house they had left. 'Nobody would venture to sell or give us peats, the only fuel used, for fear of the factors. But at last it was contrived that they would allow us to take them by stealth and under cover of night. My employment obliging me to be often from home, this laborious task fell to the lot of my poor wife. . . . Instances, however, were not few of the kind assistance of neighbours endeavouring by various ways to mitigate her hard lot, though of course always by stealth, lest they should incur the vengeance of the factors.'

The factors at this time had larger preoccupations than the obstinacy of Donald Macleod. The immense estate of Lord Reay in western Strathnaver and Strath Halladale on its eastern border had just been purchased, which presented Patrick Sellar with the prospect of mopping up innumerable *banditti*, and the factors with opportunities for almost unlimited benevolence. At the same time, nothing could hamper improvement more seriously than an agitator who was seen to have flouted their authority with impunity. The authorities showed wisdom in not overlooking Macleod among all their other responsibilities. They were also wise in their decision, as the outcome proved, that the only way to get rid of him was to continue frightening his wife.

'During the winter and following spring every means was used to induce Mr. Innes to withdraw his protection and turn us out of the house; so that I at last determined to take steps for removing myself and family for ever from those scenes of persecution and misery. With this view, in the latter end of spring I went to Edinburgh and found employment, intending when I had saved as much as would cover the expenses, to bring the family away.' Donald Macleod's absence was all that was necessary. A factor, 'bounced into my house one day quite unexpectedly and began abusing my wife, and threatened if she did not instantly remove, he would take steps that would astonish her, the nature of which she would not know till they fell upon her; adding that he knew Donald Macleod was now in Edinburgh, and could not assist her in making resistance.'

Donald's wife was frightened into making a false move. She went for protection to a house over which the factors had control, the home of Donald's mother at Bettyhill near to the parish church. 'There she hoped to find shelter and repose for a short time till I should come and take her and the family away, and this being the week of the sacrament, she was anxious to partake of that ordinance in the house where her forefathers had worshipped, before she bade it farewell for ever. But on the Thursday previous to that solemn occasion the factor again terrified her by his appearance, and alarmed my mother to such an extent that my family had again to turn out in the night, and had they not a more powerful friend, they would have been forced to spend that night in the open air.'

At this point the spirit of resistance of Donald's wife collapsed. The very next day, without waiting for the sacrament, she set out with her entire family to cover the distance of over thirty miles that separated her from the town of Thurso in Caithness, safely distant from the Sutherland estate. The journey took her two days, and although the physical hardships may not have been more severe than those of her former flitting, it seems that this time her nerves had succumbed to the strain. 'These protracted sufferings and alarms have made fatal inroads on the health of this once strong and healthy woman—one of the best of wives—so that instead of the cheerful and active helpmate she was formerly, she is now, except at short intervals, a burden to herself, with little or no hopes of recovery.'

It proved a misfortune to the house of Sutherland also, to have driven Macleod to Edinburgh. For the capital of Scotland, that strange and many-sided city, was at this time unobtrusively adding a new dimension to its personality. For too long it had been the stronghold of the English-speakers in Scotland. For long enough to attract the admiration of Europe it had been a focal point of human speculation and intellectual curiosity. Now a growing number of its citizens were becoming interested in the responsibilities of Edinburgh, not only to Europe and mankind, but to the whole of the country of which it had so long called itself the capital. They were inspecting the duties they owed to Celtic Scotland with the sudden enthusiasm which novelty so often engenders. Gaelic literature was being published in Edinburgh, David Stewart of Garth's great work on the Highlands was issued in the same city that had reared James Loch and the Countess-Duchess, and it was the capital of Scotland indeed that published the reminiscences of Donald Macleod from remote Strathnaver.

The flight to Thurso occurred in the spring of 1831, but the reminiscences were not published until after the death of the Countess-Duchess in 1839. Donald Macleod kept in close touch with the north, however, both by revisiting his native country, and by correspondence with men whose names he felt obliged to suppress, since 'utter ruin would instantly overtake the individual, especially if an official, who would dare to throw a gleam of light on the black deeds going on'.

One of his tours of the district coincided with that of the second Duke of Sutherland in 1833, just before he succeeded to the title. Macleod recorded that the Duke was equally shocked by some of the things he saw, and gave orders for their redress which Loch ignored. It did not occur to Macleod that the Countess-Duchess herself might have rescinded the order, and indeed there is something exceedingly touching about his references to the Great Lady of Sutherland, published just after her death. He recalled the expressions of pity with which she had recoiled from the effects of her benevolence, on a state visit to the north. He chronicled little acts of kindness she showed to individuals, and gave it as his opinion that she could not have been the knowing instrument of so much wickedness. It was a pity she did not live to read the most astonishing compliment that was ever paid to her. It is greatly at variance with the tradition of her hard nature, preserved by one of her own descendants.

Donald's first attempt to publish his account of events in Sutherland ended inauspiciously. He was given space for a few remarks in the *Edinburgh Weekly Journal* of the 29th May 1840, to which someone describing himself as a Sutherland tenant replied, 'denying my assertions and challenging me to prove them by stating facts'. But when Donald attempted to do this the editor refused to publish, leaving the impression that Donald had no facts to offer.

With his usual persistence Donald approached another editor, and so there appeared in the *Edinburgh Weekly Chronicle* during 1840 and 1841 the twenty-one letters that form the nucleus of his *History of the Destitution in Sutherlandshire*. While he was preparing them for republication in this form, the incidents known as the Durness riots were occupying people's attention throughout the country. Donald was able to add four letters to his history, in which he included verbatim accounts sent to him from Durness itself. For the first time, Donald Macleod the stone-mason had provided a forum in Edinburgh for the instant dissemination of the views of his countrymen.

What had happened in Durness was that a tenant from the south had 'set up as a fish curer and rented the sea to' the inhabitants 'at his own pleasure, furnishing boats and implements at an exorbitant price while he took their fish at his own price, and thus got them drowned in debt and consequent bondage'. This man, whose name was Anderson, had recently decided to speculate in sheep instead, and according to a correspondent he adopted the same method of getting rid of the surplus population that had been so effective in Macleod's case.

73

'When the whole male adult population were away at the fishing in Wick, he employed a fellow of the name of C . . . l to summon and frighten the poor women in the absence of their husbands.' But the women 'congregated, lighted a fire, laid hands on C . . . l, and compelled him to consign his papers to the flames.' Emissaries were sent to Dornoch and the Sheriff-Substitute set out under guard for Durness. The 53rd Regiment at Edinburgh Castle received orders to march. The minister of the parish in which Rob Donn is buried preached that 'all the evils inflicted upon them were ordained of God, and for their good, whereas any opposition on their part proceeded from the devil, and subjected them to just punishment here, and eternal torment hereafter'.[12]

But the sanctions of the army, the law and the Church had been undermined: or rather, they were about to pass into different hands. An inquiry was instituted from Edinburgh, and in the same city the clouds of disruption were gathering: the seventeen ministers of Sutherland would soon be without a flock between them—other than sheep.

Donald Macleod had much to console him as he nursed his incurably demented wife.

7

What the Ministers Said
1841

———◆◆◆———

WHILE Donald Macleod was publishing his interpretation
of events in Sutherland in the *Edinburgh Weekly Chronicle*, every
minister in that county was busy with the same task. Four of
them, including the Rev. David Mackenzie of the parish of Farr,
had already completed it. The published sum of their combined
labours was the Second Statistical Account of Scotland.

The First Statistical Account was the achievement of the
indefatigable Sir John Sinclair of Ulbster in Caithness. Sinclair
had designed his survey of Scotland by parishes in 1790, and by
memorializing all parish ministers for information he had
secured the completion of his invaluable work within the next
ten years. Before Sir John Sinclair died in 1835 he had the
satisfaction of knowing that a second edition was being prepared.
The Rev. David Mackenzie of Farr, in fact, had already
completed his entry in the previous year.

Few men had a more stirring story to contribute to the
second edition than the minister of Farr. In his immense parish
(forty miles from Strathy in the north-east to Mudale beyond
Loch Naver in the south-west) resounding events had occurred
in which he had borne a conspicuous part. A revolutionary
scheme of social and economic progress had been all but
completed, supported by the minister, though impeded by all
too many of his flock. What a story the minister had to unfold,
who had given evidence at the trial of Patrick Sellar in 1816, and
had helped to rid his parish of Donald Macleod in 1830. In the

75

Rev. David Mackenzie the house of Sutherland might expect to find at last a competent and reputable apologist.

But the minister of Farr shrank from this additional service to the family that had built him such a commodious new manse. He devoted more space to the supposed healing properties of *Loch mo Naire* than to the upheavals of his parishioners. 'The census of 1831, compared with the return in 1790, shows a decrease of 400 in the population,' he recorded concisely. 'This was owing to the introduction of the sheep-farming system. By its adoption the farmers and tenants who occupied the straths and glens in the interior were, in 1818 and 1819, all removed from these possessions. Allotments of land were marked out on the sea-coast for such as were thus removed. In these the greater number of the removing tenants settled; but several families quitted the parish altogether, and thus diminished the population.' The minister thus disposed of the Sutherland clearances in five sentences. He did not disclose whether they had been a divine retribution for sin, or a manifestation of God's loving providence.

He did indicate that his flock were deserving of loving providence rather than retribution. 'The people are social among themselves; kind and hospitable to strangers, according to their circumstances; acute and intelligent, according to their advantages; moral in their general habits; regular in attending on religious ordinances; and many among them decidedly pious.' What had happened to them (so barely recorded) ought therefore to have been a blessing rather than a scourge.

Yet Mackenzie suggested, in so far as he would commit himself at all, that his flock had been scourged by the God of righteousness. It is in the concluding observations that the attitude of the Gaelic intelligentsia escapes from the pursed lips of the minister of the establishment. 'When the former Account was written, a considerable number of tacksmen, natives of the parish, occupied extensive farms in different parts of it; and with them, a dense population of subtenants resided in the interior straths and glens. Now, however, all the lands, both hill and dale which they possessed, are held in lease by a few sheep farmers, all non-resident gentlemen—some of them living in Caithness, some on the south coast of this county, and some in England. And the straths, in which hundreds of families lived comfortably, are now tenanted by about twenty-four families of herds. In place of the scores of Highland cattle, horses, sheep, and goats, which formerly were brought to market, or used for domestic purposes, now thousands of fleeces of Cheviot wool, wedders and ewes are annually exported.'

The people who had lived comfortably in the glens 'are thickly settled along the sea-coast of the parish, in some instances about thirty lotters occupying the land formerly in the possession of twelve, and some of them placed on ground which had been formerly uncultivated.'

One opinion Mackenzie did not disguise. The substitution of absentee foreigners for the former leaders of Gaelic society appeared to him catastrophic. The figure of Patrick Sellar haunted the minister of Farr as it has haunted every inhabitant of Strathnaver since his arrival there, to this day.

'The lease-holders of our large sheep farms are, as was already mentioned, all non-resident gentlemen. But the former tacksmen resided on their own farms, most of them having respectable and numerous families. By their status in society, as justices of peace and officers in the army, their example in their general intercourse with the people had an influence in giving a respectable tone to society, which is now almost gone.' The social life of the Rev. David Mackenzie in the great manse of Farr was perhaps little richer than that of his parishioners, crowded in the coastal allotments.

The adjoining parish of Reay to the east lay partly in Caithness, where Innes of Sandside was one of the proprietors, and partly in Sutherland, where the Countess-Duchess owned Strath Halladale. The minister of Reay wrote with less ambiguity than his colleague of Farr about the condition of his parishioners. 'They are in general intelligent, moral and religious. The distress at present existing in the parish, however, is great in the extreme. The most of the parish has been converted into sheep farms, and consequently the poor people have been ejected from their houses and lands, many of them reduced to indigence and misery, and others necessitated to emigrate to a foreign land.' The insecurity of the tenant, to which Sismondi had drawn attention, was not glossed over by the minister of Reay. 'Leases are in fact seldom granted, which is a principal obstacle to agricultural improvements, as the tenant, who may be removed at the will of the proprietor, cannot depend on reaping the benefit of his labour. He is therefore loth to incur expenses in improving his farm.'

To the west of Farr lay the parish of Tongue. Here the minister, for all that he had been castigated by Donald Macleod for supporting the proprietor, found it no easier to justify the policy of improvement than his brethren had done. But he devised an ingenious expedient. He blamed Lord Reay for the very policy that was expounded by James Loch in his *Account*, and represented the house of Sutherland as (potential) saviours. This enabled him to write with greater freedom.

'Many changes have taken place in the parish since the former Account was drawn up. The first and most important is the introduction of sheep farming. The character of this change will be variously estimated, as persons are disposed to look at one or other of its effects. That it has rendered this country more valuable to proprietors cannot be questioned. For certain it is that in no other way could a great part of it be laid out to such advantage; though it may fairly be questioned whether, by extending it too far, they have not injured themselves. If, however, we are to estimate this system by its bearing on the former occupiers of the soil, and by the circumstances into which it has brought their children, no friend of humanity can regard it but with the most painful feelings.'

Loch had described his improvements as beneficial, not only to his employers, but no less to the native people. He had devoted pages of prophetic rhetoric to the approaching millennium. It had arrived, and the minister of Tongue painted its lineaments. 'When introduced here, several hundreds, many of them of a grade quite superior to mere peasants, were driven from their beloved homes where they and their fathers enjoyed peace and plenty. Some wandered to Caithness, others sought an asylum in the woods of America, but most, clinging with a passion to their native soil, located themselves by permission in hamlets near the shore. In these places the land, already occupied by a few, but now divided among many, was totally inadequate to the maintenance of all, and fishing became their necessary resource. And thus, on a tempestuous coast, with no harbours but such as nature provided, and in a country inaccessible from want of roads to enterprising curers, were these people often necessitated to plunge into debt for providing fishing materials,

and to encounter dangers, immensely increased by their un-
avoidable ignorance of navigation, in order to obtain subsistence
and defray their rents.'

It is inconceivable that the minister had not studied Loch's
Account (although none of the ministers admitted its existence
in their entries). By a second ingenious subterfuge the minister
affected to think the coastal catastrophe an unforeseen accident,
rather than an integral part of the factor's blue-print for
progress. He noted the gesture of the second Duke of Sutherland, made as soon as he succeeded to his title. 'His attention
was arrested by this evil, and persuaded that to reclaim these
arrears was impossible without ruining his people, he determined to cancel the whole.' The minister felt, or at any rate
expressed a feeling, of confidence in the humanity of the new
proprietor. 'After such conduct, everyone must feel that his
Grace has the interest of his people deeply at heart.'

Westward from the summit ridge of the Moine, the neighbouring parish of Durness stretched to Cape Wrath. Here the
minister wrote an entry for the second Statistical Account so
similar in attitude to that of the Rev. David Mackenzie of Farr
that it is impossible to dismiss the possibility of collusion. Both
entries were forwarded in 1834, while those from Reay and
Tongue were completed in 1840 and 1841. So it was the
minister of Tongue who was still writing when the Durness
riots took place, and the minister of Durness could congratulate
himself on the punctuality which had saved him from any
obligation to comment on events that had given his parish such
unseemly notoriety.

Like the Rev. David Mackenzie, he passed over the clearances
with unenthusiastic brevity. He remarked that the advantages
these had brought to the proprietor were not shared by the
native people. He echoed the minister of Farr's lament for the
vanished native gentry. 'The division of the parish into such
extensive farms has also suppressed almost entirely the *middle
classes* of society, who paid rents of from £10 to £50, and has
thereby tended to extinguish, in a great degree, the intelligence
and laudable emulation of the lower classes.' Among the
English-speaking incomers whom the minister presumably did
not consider a suitable substitute for emulation was Anderson,
cause of the so-called riots.

Such were the views of the ministers in the country which had once been known as Strathnaver. In Sutherland proper the country's rulers secured comment a little less damning than this timid disparagement. The minister of Kildonan accounted with cheerful brevity for the fact that his parish was diminished from nearly one and a half thousand in 1801 to a total of 257 in 1831. He had not witnessed the flitting of the remainder: it was the Rev. Alexander Sage, now dead, who had watched with so much sorrow the dispersal of his flock. His son the Rev. Donald Sage had also been an eyewitness of these events, but he had long left the neighbourhood, and for all anyone knew he had by now erased the memory of them from his mind.

The minister of Lairg expressed himself positively in favour of the changes, and the minister of Clyne, in which Dunrobin Castle stood, wrote of 'the extensive and perfect improvements on the estate of Sutherland'. But in his enthusiasm the good minister let slip an observation whose terrible accuracy he could hardly have foreseen. 'Though the country people are but little educated, they will soon discover an error in doctrine, and can quote scripture in support of their arguments with surprising readiness and accuracy. They are not fanatical nor given to prejudice, if directed by a clergyman whom they respect.' The clergymen intruded by landlords upon their tenants had not long to wait for an expression of the real opinions of their congregations.

One by one the ministers of Sutherland completed the accounts of their parishes, and so oblivious were they of the storm gathering in the south that some of them remarked on the absence of dissenters in their midst. When the Disruption burst on them in 1843 there rose up dissenters in plenty where they had sown their dragons' teeth.

What followed is described (by extraordinary coincidence) by another stone-mason from the north who had removed to Edinburgh.

While Donald Macleod from Rossal was publishing his letters in 1840, Hugh Miller was serializing in *The Witness* the geological discoveries which he published in 1841, the year in which Macleod also reissued his articles in book form. The stone-mason from Cromarty's book, *Old Red Sandstone*, instantly earned him a European reputation; and so gave his views an authority far beyond that of his brother craftsman.

Hugh Miller recalled the visits of his youth to the land whose hills had been part of the panorama of nine counties which surround Cromarty. 'We are old enough to remember the county in its original state, when it was at once the happiest and one of the most exemplary districts in Scotland; and passed, at several periods, a considerable time among its hills. We are not unacquainted with it now, nor with its melancholy and dejected people, that wear out life in their comfortless cottages on the sea-shore.'

He had watched this transition from its beginning, when Sellar started burning at one end of the strath and no provision had been made at the other end because one factor's wife was ill and another was occupied in the south. 'In the month of March 1814 a large proportion of the Highlanders of Farr and Kildonan . . . were summoned to quit their farms in the following May. In a few days after, the surrounding heaths on which they pastured their cattle, and from which at that season the sole supply of herbage is derived . . . were set on fire and burnt up. There was that sort of policy in the stroke which men deem allowable in a state of war. The starving cattle went roaming over the burnt pastures, and found nothing to eat. . . . Term day was suffered to pass. The work of demolition then began.' The crimes of which the Lord Advocate had brought no proper evidence at Sellar's trial, the tale which the ministers of Farr and Kildonan had shrunk from relating, were set down incisively in the columns of *The Witness*. The famous geologist quoted Sismondi for the first time in English translation, and cor-roborated many of the statements just published by Donald Macleod.

But Hugh Miller had a new chapter to add since the Dis-ruption of 1843. The outcome which Stewart of Garth had feared so long ago had now come to pass. The ministers appointed by the landlord were rejected by nine-tenths of their flocks, who, in their undiminished piety, sought pastors who would give them the consolations of religion that were their sole remaining treasure. 'We have exhibited to our readers, in the clearing of Sutherland, a process of ruin so thoroughly disastrous that it might be deemed scarcely possible to render it more complete.' But one fresh act of policy remained for the second Duke, which had not been open to his mother, enabling him 'to grind into powder what had been previously broken into fragments'.

The policy was expressed in two regulations. 'No sites are to be granted in the district for Free Churches, and no dwelling houses for Free Church ministers. The climate is severe, the winters prolonged and stormy, the roads which connect the chief seats of population with the neighbouring counties dreary and long. May not the ministers and people be eventually worn out in this way?' But to make certain, a second regulation was added. The penalty for entertaining or sheltering a Free Church minister was instant eviction.

Hugh Miller published several instances of the vindictive cruelty with which these regulations were being enforced. Like Donald Macleod, he seems to have been challenging the house of Sutherland deliberately to bring an action of libel if they believed themselves innocent. And it is strange to contemplate these two Highland stone-masons in Edinburgh, armed only with the truth, castigating one of the most powerful families in Europe.

One of the seceding ministers of Sutherland (Miller unfortunately thought it inadvisable to disclose his name), 'who resigned his worldly all for the sake of his principles, had lately to travel, that he might preach to his attached people, a long journey of forty-four miles outwards, and as much in return, and all this without taking shelter under cover of a roof, or without partaking of any other refreshment than that furnished by the slender store of provisions which he had carried with him'. As a warning a woman in Sutherland was threatened with eviction for harbouring her own father after he had abandoned his manse as a dissenter. And at Dornoch, where a different proprietor presented ground for a Free Church, the Duke of Sutherland prohibited the use of the neighbouring quarry, and actually ordered part of the church to be pulled down and its stones returned.

The fragments had been ground into powder, but it had not yet been pulped, and Hugh Miller did not foresee how this next process would be carried out. But it escaped his insight by only a narrow margin. 'Though the interior of the country was thus improved into a desert, in which there are many thousands of sheep, but few human habitations, let it not be supposed by the reader that its general population was in any degree lessened. So far was this from being the case, that the census of 1821 showed an increase over the census of 1811 of more than two hundred; and the present population of Sutherland exceeds by a thousand its population before the change. The country has not been depopulated—its population has been merely arranged after a new fashion. The late Duchess found it spread equally over the interior and the sea-coast, and in very comfortable circumstances. She left it compressed into a wretched selvage of poverty and suffering that fringes the country on its eastern and western shores, and the law which enabled her to make such an arrangement, maugre the ancient rights of the poor Highlanders, is now on the eve of stepping in, in its own clumsy way, to make her family pay the penalty. The southern kingdom must and will give us the poor law; and then shall the selvage of deep poverty which fringes the sea-coasts of Sutherland avenge on the titled proprietor of the county both his mother's error and his own.'

Access to accurate and detailed information had altered the climate of opinion in Edinburgh during the twenty years since Sir Walter Scott had turned his back on what he recognized as the disagreeable truths of Stewart of Garth. Perhaps it was this that made Hugh Miller over-optimistic. In fact, Edinburgh's opportunity to influence events in the north had been lost. The new Duke of Sutherland was an Englishman, his factor resided in London; and whatever storms might blow in Strathnaver or in Edinburgh, these men could well safeguard the Houses of Parliament from any little draughts that reached so far south. They were proprietor and manager, members of the Lords and Commons, immensely rich and well connected. In what concerned the sacred rights of property the truth was what they said it was. All else (and that was quite a lot by now) was lies.

Hugh Miller may be forgiven for failing to recognize a situation which still astonishes. Perhaps if he had been a reader of the *Quarterly Review*, it would have given him further insight. For this London journal reviewed the reports of the ministers of Sutherland in the second Statistical Account, and deliberately repaired their most glaring omission. It reviewed their volume jointly with James Loch's *Account of the Improvements*, published over twenty years before.

All James Loch's prophecies had proved correct, wrote the anonymous reviewer, all his designs had prospered, despite 'perversion and misrepresentation', and 'artful and designing agitators'. A miracle had been achieved by 'a most rare combination of prudence and courage, with generosity and tenderness'. It had turned a 'savage and poverty-stricken wilderness' into a garden 'guided by Mr. Loch and supported by the calm, cool judgment and unflinching justice of the late Duke of Sutherland'. Nor was his wife deprived of her mead of praise. 'The Great Lady of the Country of the Clan Chattan will be proudly and affectionately remembered in the Highlands of Scotland many a year after the graceful Countess and Duchess is forgotten in the courts and palaces of which she was for a long period one of the most brilliant ornaments.' The reviewer would be shocked if he could read the exact Gaelic words in which the Great Lady is indeed most widely remembered today.

Nothing that James Loch had written was even questionable after twenty years. Nothing the ministers had written was more nor less than gloss on holy writ. There had been no Stewart, Sismondi or Donald Macleod: only the devils who haunt Loch's *Account*. And it is precisely this devil-fixation which betrays the authorship. The self-praise does not militate against such an attribution. Loch praised himself over his own name in the *Account* in a manner that few men have ever used.[13]

Hugh Miller believed that Parliament would be compelled to intervene, just as Sismondi had done. Neither could have believed that Sutherland would be specifically excepted from relief, on the grounds that conditions there were as the *Quarterly Review* described them. But this is what occurred.

8

What Parliament Did

1845

THE fifth decade of the nineteenth century was moving towards its meridian. Hardly was this passed before the British Parliament presided over one of the most horrible acts of inhumanity in recorded history.

The exact numbers of people who starved to death in Ireland between 1846 and 1851 or who were forced to emigrate have been variously estimated, and the sincere differences of opinion over the exact figures are to be respected where conclusive evidence is lacking. But neither the Government nor the landlords can be exculpated by estimating that slightly less than a million people, rather than slightly more, died of hunger; or that not nearly so many as another million were driven from their native land.

While an annihilation of the Celtic peoples on such a scale was taking place in Ireland, it is not surprising that the sufferings of a few thousands of them in the far north of Scotland should have failed to attract effective sympathy.

The Parliament of landowners could not have been ignorant of what was occurring in Ireland, for it had been informed clearly and in good time by every known oracle. 'Now, when this misfortune occurs,' the Duke of Wellington had warned as early as 1830, 'there is no relief or mitigation excepting a recourse to public money. The proprietors of the country, those who ought to think for the people, to foresee this misfortune, and to provide beforehand a remedy for it, are amusing themselves in the Clubs in London, in Cheltenham, or Bath, or on the Continent, and the Government are made responsible for the evil. . . . Then, if they give public money to provide a remedy for this distress, it is applied to all purposes excepting the one for which it is given; and most particularly to that one, viz. the payment of the arrears of an exorbitant rent.'

In 1840 Thomas Carlyle spoke out. 'Ireland has near seven millions of working people, the third unit of whom, it appears by Statistic Science, has not for thirty weeks each year as many third-rate potatoes as will suffice him. It is a fact, perhaps the most eloquent that was ever written down in any language, at any rate of the world's history. . . . A Government and guidance of white European men which has issued in perennial hunger of potatoes to the third man extant—ought to drop a veil over its face, and walk out of court under conduct of proper officers; saying no word; expecting now of a surety sentence.'

Four and a half million pounds left Ireland annually in rents to the absentee landlords. Far more food than would have sufficed to feed its population both with meat and cereals was exported from that fertile land. But the cultivators lived on water and potatoes, and although there was never a more abundant harvest of oats than in 1845, the first year of the potato blight, the people starved. Far away in Celtic Strathnaver, Patrick Sellar was exporting his mutton while water bailiffs guarded the lochs and rivers teeming with fish, for such as the Berwick curers. Hugh Miller thought Parliament must intervene. But Parliament was turning a deaf ear to the great O'Connell himself, as he unfolded the appalling tale of his country's sufferings.

Starvation is a clumsier weapon than the modern gas-chamber; 1846 must have been a disquieting year in the clubs of London, Bath and Cheltenham, as the news filtered through. 'Tipperary in insurrection, Clonmel in a state of siege. Government bayonets displayed. The People's food locked up. Hilltops covered with thousands of strong men, livid with hunger. Provision boats boarded, mills and stores ransacked. Galway, Cork, Clare, Limerick counting their deaths of starvation. Families in Cavan resolved on a suicide of starvation to escape beggary. Thousands on thousands waiting for Typhus, or some newer or more hideous phantom to rescue them from the griping horrors of want. To this we have arrived, worse is coming.' That was in April 1846, and still the Government declined to intervene. The Queen's Speech the following January noticed that 'the loss of the usual food of the people has been the cause of severe sufferings, of disease, and of greatly increased mortality among the poorer classes; outrages have become more frequent, chiefly directed against property'. But there was no need for real alarm. 'It is satisfactory to me to observe that in many of the most distressed districts the patience and resignation of the people have been most exemplary.'

There are ample descriptions of the sights that gave Her Majesty's Government such satisfaction. 'We are here in the midst of one of those thousand Golgothas that border our island with a ring of death from Cork harbour all round to Lough Foyle. There is no need of enquiries here, no need of words. . . . Grass grows before the doors, we fear to look into any door, though they are all open or off the hinges; for we fear to see yellow chapless skeletons grinning there. But our footfall rouses two lean dogs, that run from us with doleful howling, and we know by the felon gleam in their wolfish eyes, how *they* have lived, after their masters died. We walk amidst the houses of the Dead, and out at the other side of the cluster, and there is not one where we dare to enter. We stop before the threshold of our host of two years ago, put our head, with eyes shut, inside the door-jamb, and say with shaking voice, "God save all here."

'No answer—ghastly silence, and a mouldy stench, as from the mouth of burial vaults. Ah! they are all dead; they are all dead. The strong man and the fair dark-eyed woman, and the little ones, with their liquid Gaelic accents that melted into music for us two years ago; they shrunk and withered together, until their voices dwindled to a rueful gibbering, and they hardly knew one anothers' faces, but their horrid eyes scowled on each other with a cannibal glare. We knew the whole story—the father was on a "public work" and earned the sixth part of what could have maintained his family, which was not always paid to him. But still it kept them half alive for three months, and so instead of dying in December they died in March.

'And the agonies of those three months who shall tell?' Daniel O'Connell, a dying man, paid his last visit to the House of Commons to tell their story. Perhaps James Loch had the privilege, that February of 1847, of hearing the final warning of Ireland's great leader. 'I solemnly call on you to recollect,' he concluded, 'that I predict with the sincerest conviction that one fourth of her population will perish unless you come to her relief.'

The Parliament of landowners was ready with its relief. It might be too late now to save about a million men, women, and children from one of the more horrible forms of death, but it was not too late to clear the country of an almost equal number of the residue. An Act was passed in 1847 granting relief to the able-bodied—not to the sick and aged; they could die—provided they possessed no more than a quarter-acre of land. Everywhere the starving gave up their land where relief reached them, while landlords were given every facility to complete the policy of eviction. It happened in the British Isles, little over a hundred years ago, to a number of Celtic people variously estimated within seven figures, most of whom did not speak the English language.

In the Celtic highlands and islands of Scotland, where the same policy was pursued, no Daniel O'Connell had come forward, giving up a prosperous career and refusing its highest offices, to plead for his countrymen in the British House of Commons. But Gaelic individuals had been using the language of England and lowland Scotland for over twenty years now, in their attempts to interest an indifferent public in lands as remote then as Suez and Cyprus are today. The debates in Parliament on the Scottish Poor Law give some indication of the degree of their success.

The report of a commission of inquiry had been laid before Parliament in 1843. In it the ministers who had so recently contributed to the Statistical Account gave further evidence, knowing that others in the neighbourhood were being asked for information that would be set beside their own. The report was something milder than Donald Macleod would have presented, but it was sufficient to prevent any Member of Parliament from failing to express sympathy, if not indignation: except James Loch.

The Scottish Poor Law Bill which resulted from this report had its second reading in the House of Commons on the 12th

June 1845, and was instantly attacked. The Member for Leith said: 'This Bill might have been very applicable two centuries ago.' In rural areas the parochial board which would determine relief was to consist of the landlords and ministers. 'As to the assistance of the Kirk session at the parochial board, in conjunction with the heritors, that might have been well enough when the Church of Scotland was a united body; but since the Kirk session no longer represented one-half of the people, their assistance would not be acceptable.'

The assessment for poor relief was levied partly on the landlord and partly on the occupying tenant. In the opinion of the Member for Leith this made their position on the parochial boards even more scandalous. 'The selection of the parties who were objects for parochial relief, and the extent of the relief which should be given to them, were subjects which were left in the hands of those who themselves were interested in keeping the assessment down.' There was one final enormity. The only appeal from their decision lay to a court of law, and the Bill proposed setting up a board of 'supervision' which would have the power to rule whether an appeal could be made or not. The Member for Leith pointed out that the poor were thus even to be deprived of the fundamental right of access to the law of the land.

Here is the astonishing paradox; that the Member for Leith should have attacked landlords, in 1845, in the very Parliament which remained so supine during the horrors of the ensuing years, and that he should have received widespread support. It is consequently of great interest to inspect the temper of the House of Commons as it was revealed in this debate. The individuals in the elected chamber did not reveal themselves as rogues or fools: on the contrary, they were already showing themselves sensitive to a great evil and they did not shrink either from tracing the roots of this evil to the hereditary Upper House, or from exposing the bogus arguments of a rogue in their midst. That elusive force, the collective conscience of the House of Commons, which governments have so often flouted in vain, was slowly mobilizing before the eyes of Gladstone and Sir Robert Peel.

It drew its ranks from both sides of the House and from both sides of the Border. For instance, it was the Member for the

English constituency of Rochdale who stirred the Front Bench with the scandal of Sutherland. Like Thomas Bakewell a generation earlier, this Member had been reading accounts of events in that county, and like that other Englishman he had been outraged by what he read. The accounts had been appearing in *The Times* of London and they moved the Member for Rochdale to protest that the proprietor of Sutherland was a particularly unsuitable person to entrust with the responsibilities of poor relief. Had his family not already turned a whole county into a desert filled with paupers? 'Vast districts,' he quoted from *The Times*, 'formerly thickly peopled, but now barren wilds, without a hut, a tree, or a cottage, or a wall, or any sign whatever of human habitation and industry often for twenty miles.' He added the short sentence which was an epitaph for the vanished tacksmen, the former native leaseholders: 'There is no independent middle class to speak out.'

The Home Secretary, Sir James Graham, was apparently a less assiduous reader of *The Times*, and these belated revelations in the House of Commons drew an exchange from him that reads like an echo.

'The consequence', the Member for Rochdale was saying, 'was that there was no protection for the poor; they were without hope, and the country was in a state of desolation.

'Sir J. Graham: Desolation?

'Yes, desolation.

'Sir J. Graham: In Sutherlandshire?

'Yes, in Sutherlandshire; and, if these accounts were not true, then it was quite time they should be contradicted.'

It was what Donald Macleod and Hugh Miller had been saying in print for some time.

The Member for the Northern Burghs rose instantly with his answer. But it seems that he generally required longer than this to arrange the truth in his mind. The truth with which he rose bore some relation to the one in his *Account* about all the food given to starving people by the proprietor: but there it had been expressed so felicitously that only Sismondi's perspicacity and Donald Macleod's inside knowledge had succeeded in unravelling it. Now the devils had pursued him into the House of Commons itself, and although Loch only had to repeat arguments he had used for decades, he uttered an astonishing assertion before he had properly enveloped his mind in the old arguments.

'I happen to have been acquainted with that county for the last thirty years,' he began, 'and I can say, that there is no set of tenantry in the world, that form so anxious a care to their landlord.' This was emphatic, but Loch sought greater emphasis, and he found it in figures. 'I can state, as one fact, that from 1811 to 1833 not one sixpence of rent has been received from that county.' The choice of dates is in itself mysterious. Were the entire tenantry of Strathnaver living rent-free before their lands were given to Patrick Sellar? Had Sellar himself received his vast sheep farms as a gift from the Countess-Duchess? Was Armadale a gratuity to Innes of Sandside, and was the minister of Tongue joking when he spoke of the second Duke cancelling the rent arrears among the destitute of his parish on his succession in 1833? Did the Berwick fish curers receive the Naver salmon as a bounty?

'On the contrary,' Loch continued, 'there has been sent there, for the improvement and benefit of the people, a sum exceeding £60,000 in addition to the entire rental laid out there.' On the contrary, so he explained, Sellar, Innes, the Berwick curers and all the other tenants had subscribed, not to the proprietors, but to the native people they had dispossessed, and the subscription was headed by £60,000 from the proprietors themselves. Members making a rough calculation as they listened could see that the people of Sutherland had shared over a million pounds between them during the period Loch selected. 'I could go through a great many other particulars,' he concluded, 'but I will not trouble the House now with them; the statements I have made are accurate; and I am quite ready to prove them in any way that is necessary.' He resumed his seat.

It has been remarked by many people that the House of Commons is peculiarly well adapted for assessing the quality of its own Members. Many of its most controversial figures have been at the same time the most generously admired; many of the most innocuous have failed to win respect. The judgement is a collective one, and has been said to be capable of little error. It does not always appear in the non-committal report of the House's proceedings, but it did so on the occasion when James Loch made that speech. He made it in the Parliament which turned a deaf ear to O'Connell and which must be held responsible for the death of about a million Irish people by starvation. But James Loch appears to have made his colleagues squeamish.

The Scottish Lord Advocate, whose Government's measure he was supporting, rose immediately after him. As though Loch had never spoken, as though he did not exist, the Lord Advocate referred to the Member for Leith who had criticized his measure. With elaborate politeness he apologized to the Member for Leith 'to whom he had listened with the greatest attention, as he always did to whatever fell from him', saying he must first reply to the Member for Rochdale. He next addressed himself to the Member for an English constituency on the Opposition benches. The Member for Rochdale had cited a case of eviction in Ross-shire and the Lord Advocate assured him that though he was by no means disposed to approve or to defend the system of a wholesale removal of tenants from a property of this kind— that was, where the tenantry held small possessions—yet he must say, that the result of the enquiries he had made with regard to this case were such as to satisfy him that greatly exaggerated statements had gone abroad with regard to it'.

The Lord Advocate said nothing to contradict the Member for Rochdale's statements about Sutherland. On the contrary he repeated again, 'at the same time, he did not defend this system of wholesale removal', before passing to the criticisms of the Member for Leith.

No Member referred to Loch after the Lord Advocate had snubbed him in this way: all assumed the destitution he denied: many protested against the placing of landlords on the parochial boards, the Sutherland estate remaining before the House as a warning. 'The parochial board would be solely in the interest of the landlords,' said one Scottish Member; 'the same objection applied to the inspector, who must live in the place. In the Highland parishes where would they get an inspector who was not a large tenant, and under the dominion of the landlord?' He made it clear that he referred to Sutherland by adding that the Report of the Commission 'proved the state of things in the north of Scotland to be a perfect disgrace to a civilized country'.

Thus the Member for St. Andrews. Others protested that the able-bodied poor were excluded, although they were deprived of any opportunity to work in their own parishes. The qualification of seven years' residence in the parish was condemned, so was the exclusion of the Irish immigrants from relief.

The Scottish Poor Law Bill was hurried through its committee stages as though the miseries of Scotland would be quickly cured as soon as this measure was enacted. Through the pressure of Irish Members the exclusion of their countrymen from relief was removed. The residence qualification was reduced from seven years to five years without interruption in one parish. But the able-bodied unemployed remained unprovided for, and the attempt 'to give the poor man applying for relief greater access to law and to justice' was defeated. The board of supervision was upheld.[14]

Soon the public scandal of Sutherland burst again upon the deliberation of the Members, introduced this time by the Member for Glasgow. 'Go to the county,' he said, 'of which they had heard so much—Sutherlandshire—he would venture to say, that the whole process of the management of the poor, with very few exceptions, would be found to lie in giving them only just what they could exist upon; he did not mean people able to work, but people seventy years old, some of them blind, totally helpless. The allowance to them would be found to be £2 or £3 a year. This evil had existed for many years, and the present Bill was proposed as a means of curing it; at least, the Bill went on the footing that something new ought to be done to meet the case. Yet the power was not to be put into the hands of parties other than those who held it now.' It is an extraordinary fact that the House of Commons was at this moment sitting in judgement on one of its own Members, present among them. For everyone knew it was he who had so long administered the Sutherland estate.

To this trial the Member for Rochdale brought the evidence given by the Poor Law Commissioners in their report of 1843. Loch, he said, had contradicted his statements as though they were untrue, yet they were to be found in the report no less than in the pages of *The Times*. And he quoted not only from the statements of the ministers at Durness, Tongue, Assynt, and Strathy, but also the sworn evidence of the Duke's factors at Tongue and Dunrobin.

This time James Loch was prepared. He had not, indeed, brought any evidence to refute his own underlings in the north, but he had marked those passages in the Statistical Account which in general terms applauded his administration, and he rose to read these to the House in his defence. He appears to have been a little unnerved, inasmuch as the discreet report of Hansard says mysteriously: 'Mr. Loch was understood to say, that it was with considerable embarrassment he proceeded to address the House.' But after he had read the exculpations of the loyal ministers at some length he grew bolder. He read an anonymous letter written over twenty years before by someone from Forfar who had visited Sutherland before the evictions when 'in such a state as scarcely to deserve the name of human', and after Loch had transformed it into a paradise. He concluded at last that 'he should always feel grateful for having been connected with changes which had tended to the improvement of the moral and religious education of so many fellow beings, and had been the means of increasing their wealth and position in the country'.

His satisfaction over the religious situation was something new; and extremely odd considering that most of the people of Sutherland had joined the Free Church, and were almost entirely deprived of ministers by Loch's stringent instructions. But, in fact, his arguments had by now degenerated into a meaningless patter, in which it was superfluous to distinguish truth from falsehood where there was no relevance. He spoke apocalyptically, as though he were still living in 1820, preparing and prophesying a golden future. But the future had arrived and everyone knew what it contained. Respect for a Duke and belief in the sacredness of property might protect Loch from actual interference by Parliament, but his attempts to justify himself seem to have been regarded by Members as an insult to their intelligence.

Loch had been a Member of the Commons for many years, however, and he was also a member of the legal profession, which has always supplied a large proportion of the legislature. The first devastating attack had been made on his professional and private character on the 12th of June, and as it was now the 3rd of July he had had three weeks in which to look for someone who would defend him either as a friend or as a professional colleague.

He had been almost completely unsuccessful. A Scottish

Member followed him when he resumed his seat, then the Lord Advocate, then an Irish Member, then three more Scottish Members. They made no reference to him or to the subject of his speech. But an English Member spoke next who, after giving his opinion 'that one of the greatest evils and curses under which the country had laboured was what was called the clearance system,' asked that Loch should be excused from special blame. 'It was very hard,' he said, 'that attacks should be made on his hon. Friend the Member for Wick, and the noble individual with whom he was connected; for although the clearance system had been carried out in Sutherlandshire, it had there been greatly alleviated by the benevolent feeling of the noble owner of the land in that county, and by the care of those with whom he had intrusted its management.' It was far from Loch's thesis that the clearances were an evil he had helped to alleviate, but as this was the first excuse anyone had made for him in the House of Commons, he was perhaps grateful.

Two more Irish Members resumed the debate, and then the Member for Winchester rose to speak of Loch in terms of contempt, surprising at such a time and in such a context. 'In a debate on this subject which took place on a former evening, the hon. Member for Rochdale brought forward statements, which had been made public through the Press, from which it appeared that in one part of Scotland the poor had been removed from their domiciles to a great distance. The hon. and learned Gentleman the Member for Wick then rose to answer the hon. Member for Rochdale. But he did not answer him—he only evaded the question. The same thing had been done by the hon. and learned Member again tonight. The hon. Member for Rochdale brought forward a statement as to the condition of the poor in Scotland. What did the hon. and learned Gentleman reply? Why, he entered into a long statement of the charities of the Duke and Duchess of Sutherland, and of how much oatmeal had been distributed by the Duchess among the people.

'This was the way in which the hon. and learned Gentleman thought to answer the statement as to the manner in which the people had been harassed and oppressed by being removed from their dwellings, and forced to go to distant parts, where they could not continue their accustomed occupations. This was no answer to the hon. Member for Rochdale.'

Loch's sole defender now rose. His name was Dundas, and like Loch he had risen to his present position and affluence in the service of the house of Sutherland, whose county he represented in Parliament. 'He believed that no Member of the House had taken the view of the subject which had been taken by the hon. Member,' though he did not specify which Member of all those who had criticized Loch in two debates. 'He did not think that he ought to entertain any doubt whatever that that defence—that generous defence—' (Dundas appears to mean Loch's defence of the Duke of Sutherland) 'of his hon. and learned Friend had been satisfactory to all the just and generous members of the House.'

Dundas admitted that the scale of relief in Sutherland appeared to English people to be very low. But 'it was due to the poor of that country to state this, that they sustained one another under the worst circumstances, and to their immortal honour, in their lowest state would share their last morsel with others'.

His remarks on the Kildonan clearance have the same ambiguity. 'In Kildonan the hon. Member for Rochdale said there had been a great clearance; but what said the minister of the parish, Mr. Campbell?' What neither Dundas nor his hearers yet knew was what the minister of the parish at the time of the clearance, or his surviving son, the Rev. Donald Sage, might have recorded on the subject.

When the Member for Sutherland concluded speaking, he was not pointedly ignored as James Loch had been on two occasions. The Home Secretary rose, and perhaps echoed the feelings of the House in saying that he was always pleased to listen to Dundas, but wished that he had kept silent on this occasion. And there the matter rested as the Scottish Poor Law was hustled through its final stages.

Soon it passed the Lords also, with the solemn warning: 'It was for the interest of the poorer classes that there should not be too lavish a measure of relief for the destitute poor, for by so doing, a strong stimulus to exertion was removed.' It was certainly easier for their Lordships to assess the truth of this principle than for the destitute poor of Scotland.

The debates on the Poor Law Bill reveal with what contempt Loch and his arguments were regarded in the House of

Commons. But they reveal also that the collective conscience of the House was mobilizing far too slowly for the emergency which faced it. Hugh Miller had prophesied: 'The southern kingdom must and will give us the poor law; and then shall the selvage of deep poverty which fringes the sea-coasts of Sutherland avenge on the titled proprietor of the county both his mother's error and his own.' But the new law was framed to protect him from such vengeance. For the able-bodied whose sources of livelihood were guarded by shepherds and water-bailiffs had first to be wasted by hunger before they could qualify for relief. Everywhere in the Highlands the landlords could prevent those who might become a burden to them from obtaining the necessary five years' residence; while those who possessed it already could be removed.

In 1846 the potato blight reached the Highlands. Meal rose to famine prices, and on one occasion at least it had to be carried away to the distilleries from starving people under the guard of troops with fixed bayonets. The garrison was moved from Fort George into Caithness. A Highland Relief Fund was raised, but by order of the Duke it was not admitted into Sutherland.

While there was to be no relief without work under the new Act, the board of supervision sat in Edinburgh, turning down appeals for relief that would have been heard in the Court of Session before its enactment. Donald Macleod was there, keeping careful note of them.

There was a double reason in favour of ridding the Highlands of their surplus population at this time. While the native people might become an encumbrance to landlords in their own country, their ejection into the Lowlands was most beneficial to wages there. Starvation, housing conditions, and the long hours of work in mine and factory were causing a high mortality rate, particularly among the young children who were such an economic section of the labour force. The most effective means of preventing a rise in wages was to keep the labour market constantly glutted by starving Celtic outcasts from Ireland and the Highlands. They would accept a wage that might make them unpopular with their new neighbours, but there were enough of them by now in the Lowland industrial belt to look after themselves when fighting broke out.

97

But it was precisely this interplay between the interests of the old territorial aristocracy and the industrial magnates which now began to undermine the position of both. The industrialists wanted the duty on the import of foreign corn to be abolished, either because it would save millions from hunger or because it would help to keep wages down; and were too little concerned about the effect of such a measure on the artificial fortunes of those who lived on rents from agricultural land. The landlords responded by taking an interest in the source of industrial fortunes. Already in 1842 the legislature had moved to the rescue of the children of five who sat in the dark in coal-mines for twelve hours a day, the children scarcely older who were driven by torture and terror to work for fifteen hours, six days a week. The Mines Act of that year forbade children under ten years of age to work underground in these conditions.

In 1846 Peel was converted to Free Trade. In the following year Shaftesbury secured the passage of his Bill prohibiting children from working more than ten hours a day in the cotton factories. And while Peel had split the Tory party in two over Free Trade, Gladstone had become a convert to principles that would sweep the country by his urgent persuasion.

Such was the draught that had blown through Parliament until at last it was a little wind.

As for the two German refugees who were in London in the December of 1847, drawing up a manifesto, it is unlikely that many people noticed them or thought them of any significance. The following year revolutions broke out in Europe and were quickly suppressed, and when one of the Germans retired to study in the British Museum he was perhaps hardly distinguishable from other eccentrics in the great reading-room. He found Donald Macleod's account of what had occurred in Sutherland of special interest, and noted the fact in his book. As for the remedies he proposed, over a thousand million people's lives are regulated by them today.

For the German refugee who quoted the evidence of Donald Macleod was Karl Marx, and the book in which he did so was *Das Kapital*. It was not the first book, however, in which Macleod was quoted: the first book to do this was written by an American and its thesis was somewhat different.

9

What the American Said
1854

———◆◆◆———

LYMAN BEECHER, pastor of the Congregational church in Litchfield, Connecticut, was a stern Calvinist. His children grew up in an atmosphere of piety and good works, an atmosphere suffused with cheerfulness nevertheless. When Dr. Beecher was called in 1832 to be head of the Lane Theological Seminary of Cincinnati, one of his daughters founded the Western Female Institute there, and Harriet, her younger sister, became one of its teachers.

Four years later Harriet Beecher married Calvin Stowe, the professor of Biblical literature in her father's seminary.

The seminary was a hotbed of anti-slavery sentiment, but another fifteen years were to elapse before Harriet Beecher Stowe made her phenomenal contribution to its literature. Her husband had been called, in 1850, to a professorship in Bowdoin College, Brunswick, and here Harriet was asked to lend her well-known gift for story-telling to the anti-slavery cause. The serialization of *Uncle Tom's Cabin* began the following year: it was published as a book in 1852 and sold 300,000 copies within twelve months.

Hattie Stowe was over forty years old when she found herself suddenly swept to the pinnacle of literary fame, but such was her temperament and background that the experience does not seem to have disturbed her unduly. When her novel was greeted with execrations in her own country of southern America she collected and published proofs of its general accuracy. Then she set out on her first visit to the Old World, where pirated editions of *Uncle Tom* had met with rapturous applause. The small-town pastor's daughter prepared to turn her shrewd gaze on the British noblemen, statesmen, and literary giants whose names were legend in Connecticut and Cincinnati.

Of all the functions held in her honour, none appears to have impressed her more than the reception given to her by the Duke and Duchess of Sutherland at Stafford House in London on the 8th May 1853. 'The most splendid of England's palaces has this day opened its doors to the slave,' she recorded; and if she exaggerated, so did Queen Victoria on another occasion, when she said on her arrival at Stafford House, 'I come from my house to your palace.'

Stafford House stood opposite to Buckingham Palace, on the other side of St. James's Park. 'We were received at the door by two stately Highlanders in full costume; and what seemed to me an innumerable multitude of servants in livery, with powdered hair, repeated our names through the long corridors, from one to another. I have only a confused idea of passing from passage to passage, and from hall to hall, till finally we were introduced into a large drawing-room. No person was present, and I was at full leisure to survey an apartment whose arrangements more perfectly suited my eye and taste than any I had ever seen before.'

The keen eyes of Hattie fed for the first time on Landseer, on marble Leveson-Gowers dressed as Gaels, and presently upon the Duke and Duchess who had half a dozen such fantastic museums for their homes. She found the Duchess a beautiful woman of warm and simple kindness, and the Duke a delicate man who 'spends much of his time in reading, and devising and executing schemes of practical benevolence for the welfare of his numerous dependants'. She did not mention who gave her this last piece of information.

Hattie Stowe confessed that she was flustered by the magnificence of her surroundings. 'I sought a little private conversation with the Duchess in her boudoir, in which I frankly confessed a little anxiety respecting the arrangements of the day: having lived all my life in such a shady and sequestered way, and being entirely ignorant of life as it exists in the sphere in which she moves, such apprehensions were rather natural.' If Hattie wrote this with her tongue in her cheek, she had cause to regret it later.

The Duchess 'begged that I would make myself entirely easy, and consider myself as among my own friends; that she had invited a few friends to lunch, and that afterwards others would call; that there would be a short address from the ladies of England read by Lord Shaftesbury, which would require no answer.' The few friends included Lord John Russell, the Palmerstons, the Marquess of Lansdowne, the Argylls, the Staffords, and many other members of the nobility. 'The functionary who performed the announcing was a fine stalwart man, in full Highland costume, the Duke being the head of a Highland clan.' Hattie was able to discover for herself that the Celtic race was an opulent *élite* whose leaders rivalled the sovereign herself in their style of living, while their clansmen luxuriated around them in their resplendent attire.

The little Celtic children completed the picture. 'These two little boys of the Duchess of Argyle, and the youngest son of the Duchess of Sutherland, were beautiful fair-haired children, picturesquely attired in the Highland costume.' Here was the Gaelic world of Landseer and Walter Scott brought to life in its own natural surroundings.

Escorted by the Duke of Sutherland, the pastor's daughter from Connecticut led the Highland procession through fresh avenues of enchantment towards the dining-room. 'Each room that we passed was rich in its pictures, statues and artistic arrangements; a poetic eye and taste had evidently presided over all. The table was beautifully laid, ornamented by two magnificent *épergnes*, crystal vases supported by wrought-silver standards, filled with the most beautiful hothouse flowers; on the edges of the vases and nestling among the flowers were silver doves of the size of life. The walls of the room were hung with gorgeous pictures, and directly opposite to me was a portrait of the Duchess of Sutherland, by Sir Thomas Lawrence, which has figured largely in our souvenirs and books of beauty.' Well might Hattie reflect that 'when one sees such things, one almost fancies this to be a fairy palace'.

But she kept her wits about her as she sat surrounded by 'so many men whom I had heard of historically all my life'. She noted their manners and conversation: nor did she overlook the food which was set before them. 'One of the dishes brought to me was a plover's nest, precisely as the plover made it, with five little blue speckled eggs in it. This mode of serving plover's eggs, as I understand it, is one of the fashions of the day, and has something quite sylvan and picturesque about it.'

The Stafford House demonstration of sympathy for the negro slaves of America moved elegantly to its climax. 'After lunch the whole party ascended to the picture gallery, passing on our way the grand staircase and hall, said to be the most magnificent in Europe. All that wealth could command of artistic knowledge and skill has been expended here to produce a superb result.' Hattie desribed this result in vivid detail before introducing her readers to the celebrities gathered in the picture gallery and to Lord Shaftesbury's address, with its message from the ladies of England to the ladies of America. 'We in America ought to remember that the gentle remonstrance of the letter of the ladies of England contains, in the mildest form, the sentiments of universal Christendom,' she concluded her account of this remarkable day in her life.

It was only one of a long succession of days packed with engagements in England, Scotland, and many European countries. Harriet Beecher Stowe must have possessed a strong constitution, and even she confessed later that she was forced by exhaustion to limit the number of functions she attended each day. What is evident beyond doubt is that she had no time to join Karl Marx in the British Museum, in systematic study of back numbers of *The Times*, reports of Poor Law commissioners, and the bulky columns of *Hansard*: which makes the chapter of her memoirs immediately following the account of her reception at Stafford House appear extremely odd.

Her *Sunny Memories of Foreign Lands* is a racy pictorial record of people, places, and things. Its author generally digressed into the world of ideas only when she found familiar ground. She would criticize a sermon, or discuss views on her own country that she found current in Europe. There is nothing else in her *Sunny Memories* that bears any resemblance to her authoritative statements (supported by documents of which she could not have had any knowledge before she entered Stafford House) concerning the administration of Sutherland during the past forty years.

The Stafford House chapter had ended tenderly with its invitation to American ladies to ponder the sentiments of universal Christendom. Hattie had lulled her readers only to startle them the more. 'As to those ridiculous stories,' she began her next chapter, 'about the Duchess of Sutherland, which have found their way into many of the prints in America, one has only to be here, moving in society, to see how excessively absurd they are.' The ladies of America were thus informed that the family of Sutherland was haunted by innumerable devils, who had now spread to the further shores of the Atlantic.

'In all these circles,' Hattie continued cyptically, 'I have heard the great and noble of the land freely spoken of and canvassed, and if there had been the least shadow of a foundation for any such accusations, I certainly should have heard it recognized in some manner. If in no other, such warm friends as I have heard speak would have alluded to the subject in the way of defence; but I have actually never heard any allusion of any sort, as if there was anything to be explained or accounted for.'

Poor Hattie did not even understand which Duchess of Sutherland the disseminators of perversions and lies in America were talking about. Had she found time for a moment's reflection, she must have wondered why the Duke's name was not coupled with his wife's: she must then have discovered that it was the first Duchess who had been heiress and proprietrix of Sutherland. Instead she launched into a generous and unnecessary defence of her late hostess and the Howard family to which she belonged.

If Harriet Beecher Stowe had confined her remarks to this level of gossip, it would be less easy to establish the source of her information and of her attitude with certainty. But before long she was quoting *in extenso* the speech which Loch had delivered in the House of Commons nearly eight years earlier, and supplementing it with slabs of information from Loch's *Account*, published in 1820. She cannot possibly have been allowed to read the full report of Hansard in which Loch's argument had been dismissed with contempt by Members on both sides of the House and by the two Ministers in charge of the business before it. Indeed, it appears likely that the material for this chapter of the *Sunny Memories* was handed to Hattie in the pre-digested form in which it appears, and that she only occasionally safeguarded herself with such phrases as 'the head agent Mr. Loch has been kind enough to put into my hands', and 'with regard to this story, Mr. Loch the agent says. . . .'

One passage is of particular significance. Hattie purported to give her own selection from the innumerable stories of atrocities that had been circulated. It might be questioned how she could have done the necessary research in such an immense and fugitive literature: she accounted for her choice by stating that it had happened to arrive in her mail while she was in London. It also happens to be the one incident in all Donald Macleod's writings which was brought in evidence at the trial of Patrick Sellar. 'I was present at the pulling down and burning of the house of William Chisholm . . .' quoted Harriet.

Sellar was acquitted, *ergo* Donald Macleod was a liar, and everything else he said was untrue also. What a miraculous piece of evidence Hattie had received through the post. She had shown it to Mr. Loch, who had commented: 'I must notice the only thing like a fact stated in the newspaper extract which you sent to me, wherein Mr. Sellar is accused of acts of cruelty towards some of the people. This Mr. Sellar tested, by bringing an action against the then Sheriff-Substitute of the county. He obtained a verdict for heavy damages.' It is a dreary business, inspecting Loch's attitude to truth: thus, it was not Sellar who tested the charges of cruelty in the first place, but the Sheriff-Substitute who tested the efficacy of the law by arresting him on a criminal charge.

It would have been impossible for Hattie, with all her shrewdness and powers of observation, to unravel such depths of deceit. Nor does it appear to have crossed her mind for an instant that there was any deceit to unravel. She had come to London for the first time in her life, burning with a cause that was not yet won. She and her cause had been espoused by one of the most influential families in Europe. Surely it was a small thing for a simple kindly Duchess to ask of Hattie in return, that she should defend her name from malicious rumour. At any rate, the apostle of the negro slaves accepted this strange task and supplemented her *Sunny Memories* with the extraordinary chapter on the Sutherland estate.

Hattie possessed a generous nature, and did nothing by halves. She concluded the chapter: 'As to whether the arrangement *is* a bad one, the facts which have been stated speak for themselves. To my view it is an almost sublime instance of the benevolent employment of superior wealth and power in shortening the struggles of advancing civilization, and elevating in a few years a whole community to a point of education and material prosperity, which unassisted, they might never have obtained.'

There were by now multitudes of surviving Celtic victims of the struggle of advancing civilization newly settled in Canada and the United States. Among them was Donald Macleod, who had at last left Scotland for ever, and settled at Woodstock, Ontario.

He had been in Edinburgh still when Hattie Stowe visited the city in the spring of 1853, and he had seen her at one of the public functions given there in her honour. After his departure it had been reported that he was dead; falsely, as he was able to assure her personally from Ontario. 'I know that it was reported, and circulated through the public Press in England and Scotland, that I was dead; but if even dead, it would be very unlady-like of you to attack even a dead man's character, at least until you made a searching enquiry into the veracity or falsehood of his statements.' It was indeed a severe punishment that he was still alive. 'I do sympathize with you, for I know it is a humiliating reflection for you, that for the sake of aristocratic adulation and admiration, which you could well spare, that you have exposed yourself to be publicly chastised by an old Highland Scotch broken-down stone-mason.'

Her chastisement was Donald Macleod's *Gloomy Memories*, published in 1857 in Toronto. In it he re-issued his account of 1841, supplemented by some of the as yet unpublished experiences of the host of Gaels who surrounded him in their country of refuge. In this edition he also devoted some space to the enormities of recent Irish history.

The author of *Gloomy Memories* addressed the author of *Sunny Memories* personally, and dealt severely with her pronouncement that he was an imaginative writer, and his previous book a work of fiction. 'There is thirty years since I began to expostulate with the House of Sutherland for their shortsighted policy in dealing with their people as they were doing, and it is twenty years since I began to expose them publicly, with my real name, Donald Macleod, attached to each letter, sending a copy of the public paper where it appeared, directed by post, to the Duke of Sutherland. These exposing and remonstrating letters were published in the Edinburgh papers, where the Duke and his predecessors had their principal Scotch law agent, and you may easily believe that I was closely watched, with the view to find one false accusation in my letters.'

Macleod asked Hattie: 'Can you or any other believe that a poor sinner like Donald Macleod would be allowed for so many years to escape with impunity, had he been circulating and publishing calumnious, absurd falsehoods against such personages as the House of Sutherland? No, I tell you, if money could secure my punishment, without establishing their own shame and guilt, that it would be considered well-spent long ere now— they would eat me in penny pies if they could get me cooked for them.'

Once again the embers of William Chisholm's home, which Lord Pitmilly had smoored in 1816, burst into accusing flame. 'This was a scene, Madam, worthy of an artist's pencil, and of a conspicuous place on the stages of tragedy. Yet you call this a specimen of the ridiculous stories which found their way into respectable prints, because Mr. Loch, the chief actor, told you that Sellar, the head executive, brought an action against the sheriff and obtained a verdict for heavy damges. . . . If you took the information and evidence upon which you founded your *Uncle Tom's Cabin* from such unreliable sources (as I said before), who can believe the one-tenth of your novel?'

Donald Macleod also drew Mrs. Stowe's attention to what were known in Sutherland as the Loch laws. Loch had admitted in his Account of 1820 that he had not yet found the solution to the persistent practice of marriage amongst a surplus population; what he called 'a selfish gratification of passion' where the estate did not require it. He had since extended his universal remedy to this ill, and Macleod informed Mrs. Stowe of the 'mandate of Mr. Loch which forbids marriage on the Sutherland estate, under pains and penalties of being banished from the country. . . . It has already been the cause of a great amount of prostitution, and has augmented illegitimate connections and issues fifty per cent. above what such were a few years ago—before this unnatural, ungodly law was put in force.'

Mrs. Stowe was invited to compare the circumstances of his countrymen with those of the negro slaves she championed. 'If it was possible or practicable to try the experiment,' Macleod suggested, 'that is, to bring nineteen thousand of the American slaves to Sutherlandshire and give them all the indulgence, all the privileges, and comforts the aborigines of that county do enjoy, I would risk all that is sacred and dear to me that they would rend the Heavens, praying to be restored to their old American slave-owners.'

As to Loch's pretence that his object had ever been the well-being of the Celtic aborigines, rather than the exploitation of their homeland, there was little need for Donald Macleod to pronounce on a matter so long beyond dispute. He did so nevertheless. 'I have read from speeches delivered by Mr. Loch at public dinners among his own party, "that he would never be satisfied until the Gaelic language and the Gaelic people would be extirpated root and branch from the Sutherland estate; yes, from the highlands of Scotland".'

The effects of this policy had received striking illustration during the recruitment for the Crimean War of 1854. In the lands of the Sutherland Fencibles and of the 93rd, Loch failed in six weeks to secure the enlistment of a single man. The Duke himself came up from London to Dunrobin Castle and summoned a meeting from three parishes which about 400 people attended. 'The Duke addressed the people very seriously, and entered upon the necessity of going to war with Russia, and the danger of allowing the Czar to have more power than what he holds already; of his cruel, despotic reign in Russia.' He offered a bounty of £6 on the spot to all who would enlist in the 93rd Highlanders.

There was silence, and no one came forward. 'At last his anxious looks at the people assumed a somewhat indignant appearance, when he suddenly rose up and asked what was the cause of their non-attention to the proposals he made, but no reply; it was the silence of the grave. Still standing, his Grace suddenly asked the cause; but no reply; at last an old man leaning upon his staff was observed moving towards the Duke, and when he approached near enough, he addressed his Grace something as follows:— "I am sorry for the response your Grace's proposals are meeting here today, so near the spot where your maternal grand-mother, by giving forty-eight hours' notice, marshalled fifteen hundred men to pick out of them the nine hundred she required. But there is a cause for it, and a grievous cause, and as your Grace demands to know it, I must tell you, as I see no one else are inclined in this assembly to do it.

' "Your Grace's mother and predecessors applied to our fathers for men upon former occasions, and our fathers responded to their call. They have made liberal promises, which neither them nor you performed. We are, we think, a little wiser than our fathers, and we estimate your promises of today at the value of theirs; besides you should bear in mind that your predecessors and yourself expelled us in a most cruel and unjust manner from the land which our fathers held in lien from your family. . . . I do assure your Grace that it is the prevailing opinion in this country, that should the Czar of Russia take possession of Dunrobin Castle and of Stafford House next term, that we could not expect worse treatment at his hands than we have experienced at the hands of your family for the last fifty years." '

The muster rolls of the 93rd confirm the failure of this recruitment campaign in Sutherland, but it is to Hattie Stowe that posterity owes this graphic account of the Duke's personal intervention in it, with all the other additional information published in *Gloomy Memories*. It was unfortunate for her that she should have unwittingly roused Celtic antipathies in America, in addition to the hostility of the southern states, before the anti-slavery cause was won. Therefore she deserves sympathy as well as gratitude.

It is impossible to blame her, for as she said to the Duchess of Sutherland on her first arrival in Stafford House, she was perfectly ignorant of the standards of behaviour that lay beneath the surface of those princely surroundings.

10

What the Commissioners Heard

1883

————◆◆◆◆————

IT was now fifty years since the first sheep farm had been
established between Lairg and Ben Klibreck, on the ancient
march between Sutherland and Strathnaver. What had occurred
in the great northern dukedom during these fifty years had by
now been widely and variously interpreted in newspapers,
books, Government reports, and Parliamentary debates. Many
of the events of this half-century had also been commemorated
by the people of the north in their own language, in the most
indestructible yet hazardous of literary forms, the poem that can
be memorized and sung. In this form were preserved their
feelings towards the Countess-Duchess and James Loch,
Patrick Sellar and Young, the burners of Chisholm's house and
those who occasioned the Durness riots. But no one outside the
Celtic world could see this volcano of emotion whose distant
smoke was the English prose of Donald Macleod. And if the
Gaelic language itself could be extinguished, these volcanoes of
memory might become extinct also, as Loch had so optimistic-
ally prophesied: 'The children of those who are removed from
the hills will lose all recollection of the habits and customs of
their fathers.'

By the time Donald Macleod published his *Gloomy Memories*
a watershed had been reached, but not in the sense that the
conditions of life in Strathnaver had improved, or that ducal
estate policy had been modified in any significant way. The
Countess-Duchess had died in 1839, but her son had continued

109

Loch as head factor and Sellar as mammoth tenant. Sellar had died in 1851 and his son had succeeded him. Loch had died in 1855 and his son had succeeded him as factor. A perfect continuity of management was preserved.[15]

It was in the attitude of a significant number of humane and influential English-speaking people that the watershed had been reached; and no one symbolizes this stirring of sympathy and interest better than the Lowland Scot who held the chair of Humanity at Aberdeen University.

Professor John Stuart Blackie later described a journey he had made up Deeside to the Grampian mountains in the very year in which the *Gloomy Memories* was published in Canada. 'Wherever I turned my foot in my lonely wanderings up the straths and through the glens, I came on the ruins of cottages where once happy families dwelt, whose sons and daughters, brought up in an atmosphere of moral and physical health exceptionally good, had through long generations contributed in a remarkable degree to the glory of the British name abroad, and the comfort of domestic life at home; now, as by the passing wing of a destroying angel, they had all been swept away, leaving nothing behind but dreariness and desolation.'[16]

But Professor Blackie did not linger to weep. He wrote an account to *The Times* which was published as a leader. 'For six weeks after the appearance of that number of the paper, I found my breakfast-table loaded with newspapers from all parts of the world, containing accounts of the process by which the glens of my beloved Highlands had been denuded of their natural population, and the very pith and marrow of the rural life in the Highlands sacrificed to economic theories alike inhuman and impolitic, and to aristocratic pleasure-hunting.'

Professor Blackie equipped himself to investigate this problem in a manner that had not occurred to the Highland chiefs at Stafford House or their commissioners. He learnt the Gaelic language, so that he could converse with Celtic people and read their literature. Armed with this not unimportant asset, 'I took a tour into Sutherland, and stayed six weeks at Durness. This tour brought me face to face with a yet more dreary desolation than I had witnessed in Braemar; I was now made acquainted with the heartrending details of those violent evictions in the far North which roused the indignation of that noble-minded Scot, Hugh Miller, and called forth a protest from one of the greatest economists and historians of the continent. I walked down the whole length of Strathnaver, from its desolate southern end to its northern declivity, where the extruded peasantry . . . had been huddled down to the coast.'

So Professor Blackie reached the view which marks the watershed of public opinion among English-speaking people, the view that Sismondi had expounded in 1837. It was beside the point whether this or that atrocity had been committed, and whether it had been legal or illegal. Loch's own *Account*, assuming every word of it to be true, was sufficient evidence of a state of affairs that Parliament should instantly remedy. 'I was forced to conclude that there was something radically unsound in the economy of the Highlands; and the analogy of the usurpation of the lands of the Italian yeomanry by the aristocracy in the latter days of the Roman Republic, with the consequent patriotic struggle of the Gracchi to restore the land to the people, flashed with a painful vividness on my mind.'

With statesmen of the fervour of John Bright and the stature of Gladstone to promote the same cause, it only took the Mother of Parliaments another twenty-five years to hustle towards its solution.

In Ireland there were Gracchi in plenty, but in Scotland, whose Gaelic-speaking nationals had long been in a minority a similar spirit of revolt only spluttered fitfully at scattered points. Professor Blackie believed, in the end, that the Scottish Gaels might have saved themselves much misery if they had been less law-abiding. 'The Highlanders suffered much less than their Celtic brothers, under similar circumstances, across the Channel; and, when suffering, gave much less sensible indications of their discontent than their Irish fellow sufferers. Sometimes, however, they did kick; and recent experience has amply proved that they might have been better treated, if they had at an earlier period, and with greater observance, applied to a Government accustomed to act only on compulsion from below the highly stimulant recalcitration of a Kenmare or Killarney squatter.'

The recent incidents Blackie referred to concerned firstly the Bernera rioters who resisted an eviction order by force, and were tried on a criminal charge at Stornoway in 1874. The brass plate of Innes and Mackay in Union Street, Inverness, commemorates the still flourishing firm of lawyers who secured the acquittal of the dispossessed islanders.

The second case involved rioters in Skye, and this time the men who had resisted dispossession were taken for trial to Edinburgh. 'In Edinburgh', wrote Professor Blackie, 'they could not expect much sympathy; for they had long been accustomed to keen blasts of a legal east wind from that quarter; but they were sure to find what to them, confident in the radical rectitude of their claims, was of more consequence—publicity; and even in Edinburgh, outside the range of legal formalists, economical doctrinaires, and very proper persons of all descriptions, their presence could not fail in quickening the pulses of unbribed human brotherhood.'

The men were sentenced to imprisonment, but 'whatever Edinburgh people with the narrowness of a merely local opinion might think, the crofters were not ignorant that there are men in London who live in a region far above the reach of party partialities and provincial frets'. In particular, Gladstone was in residence there, at Number Ten Downing Street. 'They knew also that the stout champions of popular rights, after years of noble struggle had at length wrung from the unwilling landlordism of Ireland some equitable concessions to the claims of a long-neglected and systematically misgoverned population; and they could not err in their expectation that the great statesman who had taken such bold steps to give to the Irish a legal footing on their native soil, would not turn a deaf ear to the more unobtrusive, but not the less legitimate, complaints of their Celtic brethren.'

The Skye crofters were convicted in Edinburgh in March 1883. The same month Gladstone set up a Royal Commission of Inquiry into the condition of the crofters throughout Celtic Scotland. Its chairman was Lord Napier, and he was assisted by Sheriff Alexander Nicolson and Professor Donald Mackinnon of the chair of Celtic at Edinburgh University. The other three members of the Commission were all Highland landowners, so that there could be little risk of undue popular bias: Sir Kenneth Mackenzie, Bart., Donald Cameron of Lochiel, M.P., and Charles Fraser-Mackintosh, M.P. The minute particulars of life in the north were to be sifted by men highly trained in distinguishing the truth, discovering evasions, and assessing the strength or weakness of memory.

The Commissioners travelled through the Hebrides during June and began their hearings in Shetland in mid-July. From there they sailed south to Orkney, and it was on Tuesday the 24th July that they began their examinations on the Sutherland estate at Bettyhill. All six of them were present in the parish church of Farr beside its beautiful bay. Behind them stood the massive canopied pulpit, so rare in a church of these parts, from which the Rev. David Mackenzie had expounded the eviction notices to his astonished flock nearly seventy years before. It had taken the Government in Westminster that long to investigate the matter, but the inquiry was to begin at last.

Delegates attended the Commissioners from Melness, twenty-five miles by road to the west, from the Caithness border almost as far to the east, and from Alltnaharra as far to the south. There were old men whose earliest childhood memories were of Sellar's first appearance in Strathnaver, young men reared on the indignities their fathers had suffered, several Free Church ministers, and a Church of Scotland minister who had decided to give the Commissioners the benefit of his advice without being delegated by anybody.

The Free Church minister of Melness was the first to be examined. 'The people feel that they have no country; that they have no right. . . . There is not a bit of ground which a countryman can call his own, or build a bothy on, from the top of Klibreck down to the sands of Naver. . . . We are in fact under an absolute despotism.' Such was to be the constant refrain throughout the county, and the minister at once descended to details of this despotism.

It was administered by a man called Crawford, who had been resident factor since 1859 for the entire area between Loch Eriboll and the Caithness border. 'What are the rules of the estate of which the people complain?' asked Lord Napier. 'That is a mystery to me,' the Free Church minister replied. 'They are called the Loch laws; and who executes them or what the code is, or to what extent they may be strained or extended or contracted, is known only to those who put them in force.' The minister, however, gave evidence of fines imposed for taking a relative to live in the house, even temporarily, without the permission of the factor; of the automatic rise in rent when a son succeeded on his father's death; of eviction; of the emigration of the young, while most of the country in which they might have won a livelihood was in the hands of foreign farmers and sportsmen.

The delegate from Strath Halladale, fifty miles distant from Melness, mentioned a man who had been banished from the estate under the Loch laws for killing grouse. The Free Church minister of Farr assured the Commissioners that the native people had been left in occupation only of the worst land in the parish. 'Do you think that the best pasture was deliberately taken for the purpose of forming the sheep farms, or was it accident?' Lord Napier asked him. 'It was deliberate,' the minister replied.

Throughout the entire area the evidence is consistent and cumulative. 'We want more arable land to give us a holding of ten or fifteen acres,' said a young crofter's son from Strathy, 'and we want also a sufficient amount of hill pasture to enable us to keep some stock. Of hill pasture we may say we have nothing; it is of inferior quality—the worst patches were given to us because they were of no other use in the world.' These young Gaels wanted their land back, and wanted to live in security under the laws of the country.

The Free Church minister of Alltnaharra was one of the first to give his opinion that the Duke of Sutherland himself would profit most, since the large sheep farm theories of James Loch had proved at last to be completely unsound. 'I have not the slightest doubt,' said the reverend delegate from Alltnaharra, 'that the Duke would realize a larger rental by placing the ground in the hands of small tenants.' The Free Church minister of Tongue told the Commissioners that this solution was the dream of the young people, brought at last so much nearer to reality by their distinguished presence in the country: 'I think it is a thing our young men are looking for—it is what they would like.'

But the young people were far from depending exclusively on the ministers of their own choosing to speak for them. On the second day of the hearing the twenty-two year old divinity student, Angus Mackay, was examined. The home of the future author of *The Book of Mackay* stands at Cathel's Field, about half a mile west of the church in which the Commissioners were convened.

Angus Mackay informed them that the parish was 295 square miles in extent and now contained 293 crofters, 'so there is enough land in the parish to give more than one square mile to each crofter.' But, in fact, 'the crofters only occupy 16½, while the remainder, amounting to 278½ square miles, is portioned out among eight sheep farmers. The crofters pay for their land, hill pasture and all, at the average rate of 1/3½d. per acre, while the sheep farmers pay only 8½d. per acre for infinitely better land; and since the last three or four years they have the land for half the rent, so that we pay 1/3½d. and they pay 4d. per acre.' This was perhaps the most succinct comment on the economic soundness of Loch's *Account* that anyone had yet offered.

Angus Mackay offered equally incisive evidence concerning Crawford's factorship. There was the case of his neighbour Angus Gordon, whose croft at Aird, half a mile to the west of his own home, sloped towards the mouth of the Naver river and the Torrisdale sands beyond. 'In 1879 a road was made through Angus Gordon's croft while a large piece was taken from him at the lower end and a lime storing house built upon it. The tenant was promised surface damages as his corn was partly destroyed, and a reduction of rent, but on making his demands when paying his rent he was only laughed at, and told that they would get plenty men to take his croft if he was not pleased with it. As he had roused the ire of the officials they gave permission to the vessels carrying lime into the river, to use for ballast the stones of the dyke fencing in Gordon's lot at the lower end. The dyke was pulled down accordingly, and now his croft is exposed to damage from his neighbours' cattle; and next year his rent was raised eighteen shillings—that was when the general rise was made on the rent—but he went to the Duke and the rent was reduced again.' Angus Mackay was asked for corroborative evidence concerning the dyke, and provided it.

Another remarkable young crofter's son who faced the Commissioners that day was thirty-three-year-old Hew Morrison from the west end of Torrisdale Bay. The future editor of the third edition of Rob Donn's collected poems was at this time a school-teacher at Brechin: he had been summoned from there to act as a delegate for his district.

Morrison showed how his own rocky coastal district of Skerray had contained twenty crofters before the evictions, and was now swollen with eighty. Some were eloquent about the destitution: Hew Morrison just used statistics. He stated that Sellar's farm in Strathnaver paid a rent of about £1,750, and explained how great the gain to the proprietor would be if two hundred tenants were settled there at a rent of £20 each. Nothing could be more proud and contemptuous than the manner in which this offspring of an expropriated race offered his terms to the Lowlanders, in their own interests.

He was followed by a man of letters of very different temperament, and if the Commissioners were beginning to feel astonishment at the contrast between people's physical circumstances in Strathnaver and their intellectual capacities, they may have wished they could have been spared this further evidence of it.

Ewen Robertson, the contemporary bard, was the son of a crofter in Tongue. His poetry has fared ill, as the language in which it was composed has gradually been forced by an alien system of education out of Strathnaver.[17] But one of his poems will never be forgotten, containing as it does his people's favourite epitaph on Sellar, Loch, and the house of Sutherland.[18]

'Have you any written statement to make?' Lord Napier inquired of Ewen Robertson, accustomed as he was by now to such timid precautions on the part of the less well educated witnesses. He soon learned his mistake. 'No,' replied Ewen, 'but I represent two districts—Tongue proper and what remains of Strathnaver; Invernaver—that is, a piece of land a short distance above the hotel. I was appointed delegate for Strathnaver, and in the first place I shall deal with Strathnaver, and if you should wish to put any questions to me I shall try to answer them. After that I shall deal with Tongue, as their case is quite different. The complaint of oppression which I have to make, as far as Tongue is concerned, is not against the present or the late factor, but against the Loch laws—some imaginary laws we know nothing about.'

Lord Napier already knew quite a lot about them. 'Deal with Strathnaver first,' he suggested. It was the last intervention he was able to make for what appears to have been a considerable time, and it is to be hoped that he listened to Ewen Robertson in the knowledge that this was the English eloquence of a man who also made poetry in Gaelic. The novelty of it might possibly have softened his exasperation.

'A great complaint of the people also is in relation to the school,' Robertson reached the point of saying at length, then changed his mind: 'but I shall leave the school for the present and shall dwell upon the amount of land in Strathnaver; and as I know it well and wrought it and examined it, I am very glad to know that your lordship is to go up the strath. You will not see the whole of the land of Strathnaver. I heard you asking why the people were turned out; a jargon was got up at the time that the people were lazy.'

Lord Napier managed to stem the rambling discourse at this point, if only for a moment. 'I must ask you to have the goodness to speak to Invernaver; that is the part of it you individually represent. . . .' Ewen Robertson replied with equal courtesy that the light he had to shed on the subject extended its beams considerably beyond Invernaver. 'Adhere in the meantime, if you please, to Invernaver. It is impossible for us to go into the general question of the clearances on this occasion.' Thereupon Ewen Robertson, having already exhausted Invernaver, passed to the other area for which he had been elected a delegate. At even greater length than before and with remarkable fluency and fervour he described a variety of oppressions in the Tongue area. The Commissioners learned about another factor and large tenant called Purves, about the poverty, the total insecurity, the immense local resources monopolized by foreigners. They left the bard to speak on until he was finished, without ever questioning him again.

The gallery of local worthies facing the Royal Commissioners in the old parish church that summer of 1883 continued to divert them with its astonishing variety. Immediately Ewan Robertson had finished, there stepped before them a man of just over sixty. His features are still well known from the portrait that was made of him at about this time and much reproduced: while his name is enshrined in the bursaries he founded for the children of the north. John Mackay had travelled up from Hereford in England to explain to the Commission: 'The good people of this district, knowing the interest I take in the class from which I sprang, elected me a delegate and sent for me to come here from England. But I am also a delegate appointed by the natives of Sutherland in Canada, New Zealand, Australia, Queensland, and Ceylon; to represent them before this Commission when it visited Sutherland. Having regard to your time now, I shall defer making any observations that I had to make to another occasion, when I hope I shall have the pleasure of meeting you in another district, and of submitting myself to any examination the members may wish.' What Hereford (as he has always been called in the north) was doing in the meantime was taking his own evidence from his countrymen in their own language. His friend Professor Blackie used it, and mentioned this circumstance.

'Where shall we have the pleasure of meeting you again?' Lord Napier asked John Mackay from Hereford. 'Very likely in Inverness,' Hereford replied; and there the brief conversation ended.[19]

The minutes of evidence were published entirely in English, and raise the question whether everyone in the area was by now able to converse freely in that language. Hew Morrison had been asked whether English was generally spoken and had answered that it was not, but that it was generally understood. The question whether Professor Donald Mackinnon conversed with witnesses in their native language, and then translated for the record, is of greatest interest when the Duke's Lowland servants were concerned in matters of conflicting evidence. The most serious of these was raised immediately after Hereford had retired.

The Free Church minister of Farr had said that the Duke's ground officer, Alexander MacHardy, had tried to terrorize an old woman into voting for Crawford the factor at the School Board elections, and had succeeded in keeping her in the house to prevent her from voting for anyone else. MacHardy was now asked: 'I would like to know whether you think it perfectly right or prudent on your part, holding the position of a ground officer, to canvas people with reference to elections.' He replied, 'I am a ratepayer and a parent, and I have a good right, I think, to speak to anybody I think proper about that. I pay £10 of rent.' He said the charge of intimidation was untrue, and that his subsequent summons of removal had no connexion with the election. Members of the family who were present when

MacHardy visited the old woman on the eve of the election deposed otherwise.

But it is the presence of the very old among the witnesses in Farr church that raises the language problem most tantalizingly. For instance, there was eighty-year-old Angus Mackay from Strathy Point, whom none but Professor Mackinnon questioned until near to the end of his examination. Is this the actual language in which they spoke, or a literal translation?

'What were you when you were a young man—were you a crofter?'

'I was worse than a crofter. I was a cottar—a slave completely.'

'What did the people of your place ask you to say on their behalf?'

'To tell how poor they were. According to my judgement they are the poorest people under the Duke of Sutherland. Strathy Point is two miles in length on one side and three upon the other. The westerly wind blows upon it, the north-west wind blows upon it, the north wind blows upon it, the north-east wind blows upon it; and when a storm comes it blasts the croft, and the people have no meat for the cattle or for themselves.'

Professor Mackinnon inquired thoroughly into the circumstances of Strathy Point, but all the time he must have been longing to ask:

'Where were you brought up yourself?'

'In Strathnaver.'

'When did you leave Strathnaver?'

'I left when young and came to Strathy Point when the sheep commenced.'

'Do you remember the time?'

'Yes, I was very nearly drowned that day.'

'Is that what makes you remember it?'

'Yes. I will remember it as long as I live. I got a terrible fright.'

Slowly and sensitively, Professor Mackinnon coaxed the distant, bitter memories from the old man.

'Were you old enough to remember the circumstances of the people at the time?'

'It would be a very hard heart but would mourn to see the circumstances of the people that day. He would be a very cruel man who would not mourn for the people.'

'What condition were they in before they left?'

'If you were going up the strath now you would see on both sides of it the places where the towns were—you would see a mile or half a mile between every town; there were four or five families in each of these towns, and bonnie haughs between the towns, and hill pasture for miles, as far as they could wish to go. The people had plenty of flocks of goats, sheep, horses, and cattle, and they were living happy.'

'Do you remember yourself quite well that these people were comfortably off at the time?'

'Remarkably comfortable—that is what they were—with flesh and fish and butter and cheese and fowl and potatoes, and kail and milk, too. There was no want of anything with them; and they had the Gospel preached to them at both ends of the strath. I remember of Mr. McGillivray being there as a preacher. But what I have seen since then! There was a beggar like myself, a woman living in Strathnaver, and she went round the shepherds; and when she came back there was one Gordon in this low country asked her, had she news from Strathnaver. "I shall tell you my news from Strathnaver." "What is it?" "The wood has been taken off the crofters' houses and it was sent to Alltnaharra for a house of revelry and drunkenness. The manse which the godly ministers of old occupied is now occupied by a fox hunter, and his study is the dog kennel. The house which yourself had, and the great big stone at which you were wont to pray, the crow now builds its nest upon the top of it." '

The Commissioners had restrained Ewen Robertson from describing events he was not old enough to have remembered personally. They now joined Professor Mackinnon in encouraging this remarkable old man as the random memories flowed back through his mind.

'You are quite satisfied yourself that these people were far better off then than their children are now?'

'Oh yes, I am quite satisfied of that. The thing that frightened me when I was nearly drowned that day was this. My father and mother and my brother went away, having got notice that if anything was upon the ground at twelve o'clock they would be fined. They rose in the morning and went away with cattle, sheep, a horse, two mares, and two foals, to the place they were to live in after, and left me and my brothers who were younger sleeping in the bed. And there was a woman came in and said, "Won't you wake up? Sellar is burning at a place called Rhistog." We got such a fright that we started out of bed and ran down to the river, because there was a friend of ours living upon the other side, and we wished to go there for protection. I took my brother on my back, and through the river I went. And the water was that deep that when it came up upon his back he commenced crying and shaking himself upon my back, and I fell, and he gripped round about my neck, and I could not rise nor move. We were both greeting, and took a fright that we would be drowned. There was a poor woman coming with her family up the strath, and she saw us and jumped into the river and swept us out of it.'

One of the Members of Parliament now intervened to ask: 'How old were you when this happened to yourself?'

'About eleven years of age.'

'How old was your brother that you were carrying?'

'Three years of age.'

'Do you know that a number of houses were burned at that time?'

'Oh! Yes, yes.'

'Many houses?'

'All from the River Owenmalloch and another river coming into Strathnaver on the east side, down to Dunviden burn.'

'Were the people very willing to leave Strathnaver?'

'You would have pitied them, tumbling on the ground and greeting and tearing the ground with their hands. Any soft-minded person would have pitied them.'

This was the place and episode of which James Loch had written in his *Account* in 1820 when he compared the ignorant and obstructive natives with 'the people of Dunviden, and of other towns in the heights of Strathnaver who, in order to facilitate a particular arrangement, agreed to quit their places in May 1818, and settled in their new lots at Strathy with the utmost cheerfulness' (p. 23). Little could Loch have foreseen that the survivors of his arrangements might one day be questioned about their experiences by a Royal Commission.

'What was the notion of the people at the time as to the real cause of all?'

'I cannot say who was the cause, but this is my opinion.

Sellar was factor, Roy was clerk, and William Young was head factor, and they had Lady Stafford under their own control, and the factors were something troubled gathering their rent. And they just blindfolded Lady Stafford and said, "We will give you £100 or £200 out of that and move the people out of the place and give the money to you all at once," and the people were removed.'

'Who got the place after the people were removed?'

'Sellar got it, but in five years' time we had a second removal.'

'Who got the place from which you were removed the second time?' 'I believe Sellar. I was in Caithness herding at the time, but I suppose it was just Sellar who got it.'

Lord Napier now spoke for the first time, and instantly extracted fresh details from the old man.

'How do you explain that your father and mother left their two sons alone in the house in bed asleep when they went away themselves?'

'Because we were weak and young, and they were sure we would sleep to nine or ten o'clock, when they would be back again. My father was back before I was ten minutes out of the river.'

'How far had your father to go; how far was the new place from the old?'

'About a mile and a half to the place called Wood of Skaill, which was an uncultivated piece of ground until then.'

'What sort of place was it; was it worse than the old place?'

'It was a place that never was laboured before.'

'Was he assisted to build his house?'

'No, he had to build his house with feal and no stone at all.'

'Did the proprietor give him any stones to build a new house?'

'No.'

'Did he give him any compensation for the old house he left?'

'Nothing in the world.'

'How long was he in this new place?'

'Five years, when he got a second removal.'

'Why did he get the second removal?'

'To Strathy Point, to the worst place there is in the district.'

Angus Mackay had not answered the question correctly, but perhaps the Commissioners noticed that he was tiring as he returned to his point of departure, for they asked him nothing more.

It was at Bonar Bridge, where the Dornoch Firth divides Sutherland from Ross-shire, that Crawford the factor appeared before them. It is clear that Crawford did not wish to speak in front of the audience of delegates who had been present in Farr church; which is not surprising, considering what he had to say. In short, that they were all liars. The man who had given evidence of the banishment of a man from Strath Halladale for killing grouse was 'very innacurate'. The delegate from Melvich was 'grossly innacurate'; the delegate from Scullomie 'quite innacurate'—in the sense of being completely so. The statements of Angus Mackay, the twenty-two-year-old divinity student, Crawford denied 'entirely'. Neither was any credence to be placed in the statements of the Free Church ministers: the one at Tongue, for instance, who was a Hebridean and thus able to converse with all his neighbours, was dismissed by Crawford as 'an entire stranger'. The veracity of the Free Church minister of Melness and of all his informants were attacked with a wealth of detail.

In any case, Crawford informed the Commissioners, anonymous persons had been advising him that the delegates did not really represent the views of the people. 'I may add in conclusion that since the inquiry at Bettyhill, I have received many verbal and written communications from the crofters, denying that the delegates who appeared there correctly expressed the true views of the population, and I am satisfied from my own experience, gained from personal communications with the tenants during these many years, that they are, as a body, as happy and contented as any in Scotland.' Such was the factor's written statement.

The Commissioners had already heard much about the Lowlanders employed by the house of Sutherland in the management of its Celtic estates, and probably they had read a great deal about them also. Now they had a sample before them. He was questioned by one of the Highland landowners who was also a Member of Parliament, Charles Fraser-Mackintosh.

Fraser-Mackintosh began by exploring the contentment of the tenantry, based on what Crawford had called a 'parental regard' shown impartially to the crofters and large tenants. Again and again Crawford was cornered by his ruthless questioning. He was forced to admit that the large tenants had

had their rents reduced for years ahead: the crofters had not. The large tenants were enabled to make large sums by subletting their sporting rights; the crofters were forbidden to do the same, though the wild game fed on their crops, and the sportsmen made free with their pasture.

Next Fraser-Mackintosh raised the question of an illegal vote of money to Crawford by the Parochial Board—a gift which he had, in fact, declined when its legality was questioned.

'Were you also clerk to that board as well as chairman?'

'I was from the beginning.'

'Did you ever hear of any other parish in Scotland where these two offices are conjoined?'

Fraser-Mackintosh passed next to the charge that a man had been banished from the estate for killing grouse.

'You stated in your paper that there were very few prosecutions for game offences in your time.'

'Very few indeed.'

'You stated that one or two were of a trifling character and others were of more importance, and because they were of more importance they were taken up by the procurator-fiscal.'

'Yes.'

'Is the procurator-fiscal not the private agent of the Duke of Sutherland?'

'Not that I am aware of.'

Finally Crawford was questioned about his anonymous informers.

'You have made some reflections upon the delegates who appeared at Bettyhill.'

'No; I made no reflections. I have simply stated that I had written and verbal communications to the effect that they did not represent the true interest and feeling of the population.'

'May I ask how these documents came to you?'

'They came by post.'

'Signed by the parties?'

'Yes.'

'Credible people?'

'Yes.'

'Do you think it a right thing for you to go and put that into your paper?'

'I don't see why not.'

'But do you think it is right in you to make reference in this important paper which you have lodged, to the testimony given by delegates duly appointed at public meetings, when you don't mention the names of those who question what the delegates said?'

'I don't see anything wrong in it for my part.'

'You allow a man or men privately and secretly to attack what the delegates said in public?'

'I am quite willing to lay the letters I have received before the commission.'

But no one asked for them: they wanted nothing more from Crawford. Professor Donald Mackinnon had not attended the hearing at all, and Lord Napier had preserved silence throughout. The factor who looked upon himself as the trusted father of the people who had expressed such execration for him from Melness to Caithness retired from the presence of Her Majesty's Commissioners. The old formulae had failed at last.

11

What Was in the Secret Diary
1889

THE report and hearings of the Napier Commission were the trumpets which demolished the walls of Jericho that landlordism had thrown round the Parliament at Westminster. 'Inch by inch, as in their Irish policy,' wrote Professor Blackie, 'they conceded to the clamour of agitation what should have been suggested by the claims of justice; and if they earned little gratitude for their concessions, they ought to be conscious that they got just what they deserved.' In 1886 the Bill was enacted which gave to the people of the Highlands and Islands protection in the lands they occupied, as statutory tenants. In what little land remained in their hands the Celtic people of Scotland obtained in 1886 the security that the Indian peasant enjoyed under British rule, that most Scandinavian peasants had always enjoyed, that had been conceded to the Prussian serf in the eighteenth century. The power of the factor, based on the threat of instant eviction, was destroyed. It was exactly seventy years since Patrick Sellar had been acquitted in Inverness.

Although Blackie had paid particular attention in his inquiries and his writings to the case of Sutherland, and although he had spoken without restraint of those landlords who 'combined the harshness of the Oriental despot with the meanness of a local attorney', he was careful to exempt the Duke of Sutherland himself from stricture. 'I have to return my special thanks,' he wrote in 1884, 'to his Grace the Duke of Sutherland, and his Commissioner, Sir Arnold Kemball, for the kind manner in which they opened their views to me on this subject.' Blackie also published details of the plans to reclaim Sutherland and resettle its inhabitants, which were discussed during that year with the Duke's approval.

This was the third Duke, an Englishman whose father was a Leveson-Gower and his mother a Howard. In politics he held Liberal views. He had inherited his title and property in 1861, and was thus the first to succeed, wholly independent of the Edinburgh management established by his grandmother Elizabeth Gordon. Whether he had any suspicions of the dregs of this administration surviving on the north coast in the persons of such men as Crawford, Purves, and MacHardy can only be surmised. What is beyond question is that steps were already under discussion to mend matters a year after the Betty-hill hearings, and two years before the Crofters' Act was passed.

Men were moving, it seemed, into a new era in which ancient wrongs, once righted, might be laid to rest; in which the behaviour of people who were now dead, whether benevolent or evil, might cease to be associated with their descendants, who were not accountable for them. Such were Professor Blackie's feelings when he wrote: 'It is not the person or persons who were actors in that business, but the policy of the proceeding which possesses any interest for me. In all my public appearances, whether as a writer or a speaker, I have systematically avoided personalities; and with regard to the Sutherland clearances, from the first time that I visited Strathnaver and wept over the ruins of the deserted cottages there, I studiously avoided introducing the name of Patrick Sellar.'

Such were not the feelings of Sellar's son and heir, to whom Blackie privately addressed those words. Thomas Sellar, of Hall Grove, Bagshot, Surrey, began bombarding Blackie with letters through an Edinburgh lawyer shortly before the Napier Commission was appointed. He likewise bombarded Alexander Mackenzie in Inverness, the editor of the *Celtic Magazine* who had recently published his *The Highland Clearances*, containing excerpts from Stewart of Garth, Donald Macleod, and Hugh Miller.

Thomas Sellar was satisfied, from the reports of Lowland travellers, that the condition of the Celtic people before his father's arrival in the Highlands was 'such as no language could describe'. The only reliable evidence for what had occurred subsequently was contained in the report of his father's trial, Loch's *Account*, and the address of gratitude to the Countess-Duchess from her devoted tenantry. Of Donald Macleod he said: 'It would have seemed almost incredible that statements of such a nature and by such a man should obtain credence.' Of Hugh Miller the geologist he said: 'It was in consistence with the character of the man that he never stopped to enquire whether the narrative of Macleod was an accurate or authentic narrative.' Alexander Mackenzie he accused of 'studied unfairness and deception'. Blackie he accused of deliberate bad faith. The corroborative evidence these men had used, the reports of Commissioners, of *The Times* and other newspapers, of the second *Statistical Account* were ignored as though they did not exist.

Thomas Sellar published this defence of his father in 1883, a year before the Napier Commission reported to Parliament using these words: 'The history of the economical transformation which a great portion of the Highlands and Islands has during the past century undergone does not repose on the loose and legendary tales that pass from mouth to mouth; it rests on the solid basis of contemporary records, and if these were wanting, it is written in indelible characters on the surface of the soil. . . . The crofter of the present time has through past evictions been confined within narrow limits, sometimes on inferior and exhausted soil. He is subject to arbitrary augmentations of money rent, he is without security of tenure.' The great sheep farms, such as Thomas Sellar's father had carved out for himself, were condemned by the Commissioners as a great mistake on economic, apart from humanitarian, grounds.

But while Thomas Sellar published his father's defence before the Napier Commission's report, others did so in a more subtle and effective manner after it. The entry for the first Duke of Sutherland in the *Dictionary of National Biography* offers the assurance: 'The stories, however, of ruthless evictions and banishment of peasants appear to have no good foundation.' And the august gallery of British worthies includes James Loch himself, with the further explanation: 'The stories of cruel evictions have never been proved, and the economic policy has been ably defended.'

If the *Dictionary of National Biography* had admitted every Member of Parliament, lawyer, or factor to its columns it would spill over many shelves. If it included every large sheep farmer few libraries would house it. Yet there, too, is Patrick Sellar, justified by his grandson Andrew Lang: 'In consequence of the periodical failure of the crops in the strath or river valleys, the crofters were removed to settlements on the coast.' Sellar had merely performed a rescue operation.

The *Scots Peerage* mentions the gratitude of the rescued people. 'The latter in some places were much opposed to the improvements, but after these were carried out between 1811 and 1826 the thanks of the tenantry were expressed to the Earl and Countess.' The date 1826 is as surprising as the designation of the Marquess of Stafford, who was for six months Duke of Sutherland: The Editor of *The Scots Peerage* was the Lord Lyon King of Arms in Edinburgh.

According to the great compilations in which the wise men of the day have commemorated its leaders, Thomas Sellar was right. Donald Macleod, then, was one of this country's great fabulists and his fictions so impressed themselves on the minds of his countrymen that they were repeated as facts in all parts of the world, and succeeded in hoodwinking intelligent men in this land for generations.

But what of Donald Sage's diary; was that also a fabrication?

None but a few relatives and neighbours knew that the son of Alexander Sage, minister of Kildonan until his death in 1824, had kept a journal of his life in Sutherland. It was all very long ago. Donald Sage himself had died in 1869, and he had left Sutherland by 1820. Only a few old men like Angus Mackay at Strathy Point remained alive to recall those far-off times, when the *Memorabilia Domestica* of Donald Sage was published in 1889.

Unlike any other account from that time and place, Sage's journal is above suspicion of having been designed as a piece of advocacy. He wrote these pages, as he remarked in them, 'not with the slightest desire or expectation that they should be published when the hand that now writes them shall be stiff in death'. His frankness about his own colleagues and relatives made it impossible that they should be published earlier.[20]

The journal (although it was not published in full) is a

tapestry in *petit point*, an intricately detailed description of domestic life in the north of Scotland extending to over four hundred pages. It begins: 'My grandfather, Eneas Sage, was born on the 12th of March, 1694,' and from his grandfather's time to his own the journal becomes a progressively richer mine of information. Page 240 has been reached before there is any mention of the Sutherland evictions.

Donald Sage desribed how he fell ill during 1813 in his father's manse at Kildonan, shortly after returning from a visit to Bettyhill. Dr. Rainy, the future Professor of Forensic Medicine and a native of Sutherland, happened to be visiting the Sages at the time. 'Harry Rainy was then a student of medicine, very talented and very argumentative. My case was by my stepmother brought under his notice. In the art of healing the sick, the lovers of it in every successive age have fancied that they have attained to the acme of perfection. The advance of the science then reached was, that the sprinkling of cold water in cases of fever was a sovereign antidote; and I was accordingly, by Mr. Harry Rainy's prescription and manual operation, subjected to that newfangled treatment.' Sage mentioned that the only doctor in the county was Dr. Ross at Cambusmore.

Immediately Donald Sage recovered, he went to the home of Robert Mackid the Sheriff-Substitute, on the east coast of Sutherland, to act as private tutor to his family. It consisted of three sons and three daughters, and Sage remained with them for a year, climbing to the top of Beinn a' Bhraggie every morning before starting work.

It was at this time, he recorded, that the clearances began. 'This sweeping desolation extended over many parishes, but it fell most heavily on the parish of Kildonan. It was the device of one William Young, a successful corn-dealer and land-improver. He rose from indigence, but was naturally a man of taste, of an ingenious turn of mind, and a shrewd calculator. . . . Young had as his associate in the factorship a man of the name of Sellar, who acted in the subordinate capacity of legal agent and account-ant on the estate, and who, by his unprincipled recklessness in conducting the process of ejectment, added fuel to the flame.'

But Donald Sage was soon to witness more sweeping desolation in his own parish than he had seen in his father's. The minister of the parish of Farr died, and in May 1815 the missionary at Achness, the Rev. David Mackenzie, was appointed to the manse at Bettyhill in his place. At the age of twenty-five the Rev. Donald Sage received his first charge as the new missionary at Achness beside Loch Naver. His salary was £50.

'The mission at Achness was, in regard to locality and surface, of very great extent. . . . A very considerable portion of the population had already been removed by the Stafford family, and their tenements given to sheep farmers, so that the peopled part of that vast district was comparatively limited. The whole population in the Strathnaver district lay apart from the missionary's house, being divided from it by the Naver, a river of such volume and breadth in the winter months as completely to preclude the attendance of the people at their wonted place of worship during that season.' The other main group of people lived in the Badenloch neighbourhood to the east, within the parish of Kildonan. Sage found he had to preach to the two congregations separately.

There were two churches at Sage's disposal, neither of which impressed him greatly. Of the church at Achness he wrote: 'When I entered on the duties it was in a woefully dilapidated state, but it was soon afterwards repaired by the people, and made merely habitable. It consisted of a long low house, with a large wing stretching out from the north side of it. The walls were built of stone and clay, the roof covered with divot and straw, and the seats were forms set at random, without any regularity, on the damp floor.' The congregation was wasting its labours in repairing this church, of which such pitiful traces survive today.

Sage described the evictions that had occurred in his parish nearly a year before he was called to it. 'A vast extent of moorland within the parishes of Farr and Kildonan was let to Mr. Sellar, factor for the Stafford family, by his superior, as a sheep or store farm; and the measure he employed to eject the poor, but original, possessors of the lands was fire. At Rhimisdale, a township crowded with small tenants, a corn-mill was set on fire in order effectually to scare the people from the place before the term for eviction arrived. Firing or injuring a corn-mill, on which the sustenance of the lieges so much depends, is

or was by our ancient Scottish statutes punishable by imprisonment or civil banishment, and on this point of law Mr. Sellar
was ultimately tried . . . but the final issue of it was only what
might have been expected.'

Some months after the trial, in the fall of 1816, Donald Sage
moved into the manse at Achness. 'Its walls were of stone and
lime. It was thatched with divot and straw and contained four
apartments, a kitchen in an outer wing, a parlour with a bed in
the wall, a closet, and a bedroom.' Some of its furniture Sage
brought from his father's manse in Kildonan, some he bought at
the auction of Robert Mackid's possessions after Sellar had
ruined him.

The seventh and last missionary at Achness spent three
years in that house, and those three years have given to posterity
a priceless record of the society, so immemorially old, which was
on the verge of such utter destruction. There was 'William
Mackay, commonly called Achoul, from the farm on the banks of
Loch Naver which he and his progenitors of the Clan Abrach
had for many generations possessed.' (The Abrach branch of
the Mackays is its earliest historical sept, and it is its distinction
to have preserved the earliest of all clan banners.) 'In recounting
to me the incidents of his life, he said he was about eighteen
years of age during the rebellion of 1745. He had been sent on
some errand to Dunrobin Castle, and being permitted to look
into the room where the Countess of Sutherland sat, entertaining
two of her noble relatives who were of the prince's party, he
noticed one of them (he was told it was Lord Elcho) with a stick
in his hand attempting to demolish a print of the elector of
Hanover which hung upon the wall.'

Achoul had been evicted in the first clearance, but had found
another home in the locality. 'There his wife died, and he laid
her lifeless remains in the churchyard at Achness. As he took his
last look of the rapidly disappearing coffin, "Well, Janet," said
he, "the Countess of Sutherland can never flit you any more." '

At Badenloch was the son of Donald Matheson, who had been
'a poet, and composed a number of spiritual songs which his son
Samuel printed and circulated'. Donald Matheson was contemporary with Strathnaver's greatest poet, Rob Donn Mackay.
'They met, it is said, at a friend's house, and each sang one of his
own songs. When they had concluded, Donald submitted his

song to the judgment of the Reay Country bard. "Donald," answered Rob, "there is more of poetry in my song, and more of piety in yours." ' Sage mentioned that Donald Matheson's son Samuel 'was also a self-taught mediciner and surgeon, and in many cases was most miraculously successful. He died at Griamachdary in 1829.' It becomes a little less surprising that this country reared Professor Rainy.

Donald Sage descended from ministers both on his father's side and on his mother's, whose family were Mackays. So it is natural that his portrait gallery should be crowded with ministers. Those at Durness are of particular interest because it was a son of one of them who published the first collection of Gaelic airs in 1784, and the daughter of another who made a collection of Rob Donn's poetry before his death in 1778. Her sister married William Findlater, the minister at Durness in Sage's time and preserver of Rob Donn's manuscript. 'This was not a happy marriage,' Sage confided to his journal, 'but he found it turn to his spiritual advantage in the decided progress which, through manifold afflictions, he was enabled to make in the Christian life.'

Few indeed could have been allowed to read such a candid document. 'Mrs. Mackay of Skerray was one of my earliest acquaintances. . . . My father and she being related through the Kirtomy family of the Mackays, a friendly intercourse was always kept up between us, and I have been a guest at her house both before I went to Achness and very frequently afterwards'. He would not have been if she had got a peep at his journal. 'Mrs. Mackay of Skerray was a pious woman, and lived in habits of strictest Christian intimacy with those who were most distinguished for their spiritual attainments. She perhaps overmuch imbued her conversation with religious sentimentalism, and often mistook the marvellous or the romantic for the higher walks of spirituality. Whilst she sincerely wished to be the companion of those only who feared God, she was not a little ambitious also of being the fine lady among them. Mrs. Mackay is still alive at Skerray, having attained to very advanced age.' Perhaps the past tense indicates a spiritual reformation after the penultimate sentence.

It was not a cloistered or isolated world that Sage described. Apart from the returned soldiers there were people who had travelled to the ends of the earth, women as well as men, although this was more rare. Amongst his Badenloch parishioners was a Lieutenant Gunn who had married a 'woman of colour, daughter of Mr. Harry Bruce, a West Indian planter, by whom he got some money, which was soon dissipated'. In the final clearance of 1819 the Sutherland estate had to compensate Gunn for his removal, because he possessed a lease.

'It was while my sister Elizabeth and I were residing at Achness that we first became acquainted with Mr. Finlay Cook, minister of Reay. . . . He came to Achness on a visit to see my sister who, in little more than a year after, became his wife.' Sage had much to learn from his brother-in-law in conversation, for 'when licensed to preach Mr. Cook was appointed to the Highlanders at the Lanark Mills by that strange visionary Robert Owen'. But Sage commented severely upon his Gaelic: 'He rigidly adheres to the dialect of his native district, the Isle of Arran, one of the worst dialects in Scotland.'

There was an occasional fuss over the appointment of ministers by patronage, and Sage mentioned the presentation of Murdoch Cameron at Creich. It reads like an episode from the novels of John Galt. 'I have a distinct recollection of his induction. The people, to a man, were opposed to him, and his settlement was one of those violent ones which so much disgraced the Established Church at that period. The parishioners rose *en masse* and barred the church against the presbytery, so that the Sutherland Volunteers, under the command of Captain Kenneth Mackay of Torboll, were called out to keep the peace. In the riot which ensued, Captain Mackay got his sword, which he held naked in his hand, shivered to pieces by stones thrown at him by an old woman over seventy years of age. The people never afterwards attended Mr. Cameron's ministry, but assembled at the rock of Migdol and on the banks of the lake, to hear old Hugh Mackenzie.'

Two personal actions of the Countess-Duchess receive comment in the journal, the one favourable, the other critical. The first of these concerned a Mrs. Mackay of Cape Wrath, known as *Bean a' chreidimh mhóir*, the woman of great faith. 'The late Duchess of Sutherland ever regarded those really influenced by the truth with the deepest veneration. On one of her summer rambles in the Reay Country, Mrs. Mackay was introduced to her at Tongue, and the interview much impressed the Duchess in favour of her new acquaintance. As a mark of her esteem, she granted to Mrs. Mackay and to her husband a free life-rent of the house and lot of land which they occupied in Melness.'

But a different dispensation was soon to occupy the minister's recording pen. 'I can yet recall to memory the deep and thrilling sensation which I experienced as I sat at the fireside in my rude little parlour at Achness, when the tidings of the meditated removal of my poor flock first reached me from headquarters. It might be about the beginning of October 1818. A tenant from the middle of the strath had been to Rhives, the residence of Mr. Young the commissioner, paying his rent. He was informed, and authorized to tell his neighbours, that the rent for the half-year, ending in May 1819, would not be demanded, as it was determined to lay the districts of Strathnaver and Upper Kildonan under sheep.

'This intelligence when first announced was indignantly discredited by the people. Notwithstanding their knowledge of former clearances, they clung to the hope that *Ban mhorair Chataibh* would not give her consent to the warning as issued by her subordinates, and thus deprive herself of her people, as truly a part of her noble inheritance as were her broad acres.

'But the course of a few weeks soon undeceived them. Summonses of ejectment were issued and despatched all over the district. These must have amounted to upwards of a thousand, as the population of the Mission alone was 1,600 souls, and many more than those of the Mission were ejected. . . . Having myself, in common with the rest of my people, received one of these notices, I resolved that, at the ensuing term of Martinmas, I would remove from Achness and go once more permanently to reside under my father's roof, although I would at the same time continue the punctual discharge of my pastoral duties among the people till they also should be removed.'

Next spring began the events that inspired Donald Macleod (unless he was telling the truth) to his most brilliant flights of imaginative writing. 'It was in the month of April,' wrote Sage in his more private record, 'and about the middle of it, that they were all, man, woman and child, from the heights of Farr to the mouth of the Naver, on one day, to quit their tenements and go—many of them knew not whither. For a few, some miserable patches of ground along the shores were doled out as lots, without aught in the shape of the poorest hut to shelter them. Upon these lots it was intended that they should build houses at their own expense, and cultivate the ground, at the same time occupying themselves as fishermen, although the great majority of them had never set foot on a boat in their lives.

'Thither, therefore, they were driven at a week's warning. As for the rest, most of them knew not whither to go unless their neighbours on the shore provided them with a temporary shelter; for on the day of their removal they would not be allowed to remain, even on the bleakest moor and in the open air, for a distance of twenty miles around.'

On the two Sundays preceeding the day of removal, the minister preached for the last time to his two congregations. 'In Strathnaver we assembled for the last time at the place of Langdale where I had frequently preached before, on a beautiful green sward overhung by Robert Gordon's antique romantic little cottage on an eminence close beside us. The still-flowing waters of the Naver swept past us a few yards to the eastward. The Sabbath morning was unusually fine and mountain, hill and dale, water and woodland, among which we had so long dwelt, and with which all our associations of home and native land were so fondly linked, appeared to unite their attractions to bid us farewell.

'My preparations for the pulpit had always cost me anxiety, but in view of this sore scene of parting they caused me pain beyond endurance. . . . The service began. The very aspect of the congregation was of itself a sermon, and a most impressive one. Old Achoul sat right opposite to me. As my eye fell upon his venerable countenance, bearing the impress of eighty-seven winters, I was deeply affected, and could scarcely articulate the psalm.

'I preached and the people listened, but every sentence uttered and heard was in opposition to the tide of our natural feelings which, setting in against us, mounted at every step of our progress higher and higher. At last all restraints were compelled to give way. The preacher ceased to speak, the people to listen. All lifted up their voices and wept, mingling their tears together. It was indeed the place of parting, and the hour. The greater number parted never again to behold each other in the land of the living.'

Donald Sage's description of some of the atrocities that accompanied the clearance, and of Patrick Sellar's direct responsibility for them, is extremely precise.

'The middle of the week brought on the day of the Strathnaver clearance. It was a Tuesday. At an early hour of that day Mr. Sellar, accompanied by the Fiscal, and escorted by a strong body of constables, sheriff-officers and others, commenced work at Grummore, the first inhabited township to the west of the Achness district. Their plan of operations was to clear the cottages of their inmates, giving them about half an hour to pack up and carry off their furniture, and then set the cottages on fire. To this plan they ruthlessly adhered, without the slightest regard to any obstacle that might arise while carrying it into execution.

'At Grumbeg lived a soldier's widow, Henny Munro. She had followed her husband in all his campaigns, marches and battles, in Sicily and in Spain. . . . After his death she returned to Grumbeg, the place of her nativity, and as she was utterly destitute of any means of support, she was affectionately received by her friends, who built her a small cottage and gave her a cow and grass for it. The din of arms, orders and counter-orders from headquarters, marchings and counter-marchings and pitched battles, retreats and advances, were the leading and nearly unceasing subjects of her winter evening conversations. She was a joyous, cheery old creature; so inoffensive moreover, and so contented, and brimful of good-will, that all who got acquainted with old Henny Munro could only desire to do her a good turn.'

At the trial of Patrick Sellar exactly three years earlier it had been established that a bed-ridden woman over ninety years old had been turned out of her home, and that she had died five days later in an outhouse. This was not contested in court, the judge and jurors apparently agreeing that Sellar could not be held responsible for the natural tendency of old people to die if rendered suddenly homeless. And there can be little doubt that this judicial attitude helped Sellar now to solve the tiresome problems of all the old people living in upper Strathnaver.

When he had cleared Grummore, Sellar came to the widow's house at Grumbeg. 'Henny stood up to plead for her furniture— the coarsest and most valueless that well could be, but still her earthly all. . . . She was told with an oath'—other accounts mention Sellar's partiality for oaths—'that if she did not take her trumpery off within half an hour it would be burned. The poor widow had only to task the remains of her bodily strength, and address herself to the work of dragging her sheets, beds, presses and stools out at the door, and placing them at the gable of her cottage. No sooner was her task accomplished than the torch was applied, the widow's hut, built of very combustible material, speedily ignited and there rose up rapidly, first a dense cloud of smoke, and soon thereafter a bright red flame. The wind unfortunately blew in the direction of the furniture and the flame, lighting upon it, speedily reduced it to ashes.'

A worse fate awaited the mother-in-law of Samuel Matheson, whose father had once discussed poetry with Rob Donn. She lived at Rhimisdale, where today only a keeper's house stands in the surrounding wilderness, and 'had been reduced to such a state of bodily weakness that she could neither walk nor lie in bed. She could only, night and day, sit in her chair; and having been confined for many years to that posture, her limbs had become so stiff that any attempt to move her was attended with acute pain. . . . In her house I have held diets of catechizing and meetings for prayer, and been signally refreshed by her Christian converse.'

Many people represented to Sellar the special difficulty of removing *Bean Raomasdail*. They were told that 'she must immediately be removed by her friends, or the constables would be ordered to do it. The good wife of Rhimisdale was, therefore, raised by her weeping family from her chair and laid on a blanket, the corners of which were held up by four of the strongest youths in the place. All this she bore with meekness, and while the eyes of her attendants were streaming with tears, her pale and gentle countenance was suffused with a smile. The change of posture and the rapid motion of the bearers, however, awakened a most intense pain, and her cries never ceased till within a few miles of her destination, when she fell asleep.'

A week later Donald Sage travelled through his former parish on his way from Kildonan to Tongue. 'The banks of the lake and the river, formerly studded with cottages, now met the eye as a scene of desolation. Of all the houses the thatched roofs were gone; but the walls, built of alternate layers of turf and stone, remained. The flames of the preceding week still slumbered in their ruins, and sent up into the air spiral columns of smoke; whilst here a gable and there a long side-wall, undermined by the fire burning within them, might be seen tumbling to the ground, from which a cloud of smoke, and then a dusky flame, slowly sprang up. The sooty rafters of the cottages, as they were being consumed, filled the air with a heavy and most offensive odour.'

What was lost in this holocaust? Not the Abrach Mackay banner, that oldest of clan standards with the Gaelic injunction *Bi Treun*—Be Steadfast—sewn into it. This talisman appears to have been carried for safety to Caithness, and now rests in the National Museum of Antiquities at Edinburgh. Two manuscript collections of the ancient herioc ballads escaped, one of which, written down in 1739, anticipated by so long the work of other collectors. Specimens of the early-seventeenth-century religious poet Alexander Munro survived in a Ross-shire manuscript of the same century. Some of the poems of John Mackay of Mudale were rescued and published in anthologies in 1835 and 1851.

It was Professor Blackie who found out and recorded what had happened at Mudale. As this was not unlike the experience of Achness, the recovery of any of the poems which had so impressed Dugald Buchanan in the eighteenth century is sufficiently extraordinary. Meanwhile the Rob Donn manuscripts were safe.

There can be little doubt that the sympathy and hospitality of the people in neighbouring Caithness saved many lives and many possessions. In Thurso lived Robert Mackay, whose *History of the House and Clan of Mackay*, published in 1829, was the first attempt by a native of the area to disprove the slanders of Lowland historians concerning the known history and supposed habits of his race. It also set a fashion for clan histories that has not abated.

But who can say what was lost of his country's records and literature by 1829? Loch wrote in his *Account* that the language of the country was one in which nothing was ever written: and it is hard to determine whether he and Sellar were ignorant enough to believe this, or whether they set out to make it true by destroying all contrary evidence. A specimen of Gaelic prose, written by a Mackay in Strathnaver in *c.* 1725, has been discovered recently in Australia to mock them. But there is little solace in such faint mockery.*

As for the minister whose private journal has mocked them at last, Sage accepted an appointment to the Gaelic chapel in Aberdeen, and from there moved to Resolis in Ross-shire. The remaining hundred and fifty published pages of his memoirs contain only a single passing reference to the Sutherland evictions.

These memoirs were published four years before the entries concerning Sellar, Loch, and the first Duke of Sutherland appeared in the *Dictionary of National Biography*, and over twenty years before the eighth volume of the *Scots Peerage*. So it can only be assumed that all the learned Lowland Scots who contributed their views to these authoritative volumes must have decided that Donald Sage also was a liar. The Lord Lyon King of Arms and Andrew Lang were apparently agreed that the minister of Resolis possessed this secret vice: that he liked to make up lies very privately, for the entertainment—or perhaps even to test the powers of detection—of God.

* *Scottish Gaelic Studies*, ix.

12

The Last Word

1905

———◆◆◆◆———

Donald sage's description of his churches, of his manse, and of the homes of his parishioners is not inconsistent with the more opprobrious descriptions of Loch and Sellar. The contrast is largely one of emphasis. These two Lowland lawyers came fresh from the elegant surroundings of the Athens of the North, and they may be pardoned for the distaste with which they described the thatched black-houses of a remote rural area. At the same time they invite comparison with the young Englishman of their day who came to Edinburgh for his university education because he belonged to a family of religious dissenters.

Henry Holland made a visit to Iceland at about the same time that Loch and Sellar first set eyes on Celtic Sutherland, and Iceland was no more strange to an Englishman from Cheshire than the Gaelic Highlands were to a Scottish Lowlander—as Sellar himself conceded when he called them a *terra incognita*. Henry Holland wrote to Maria Edgeworth,* remarking on the primitive simplicity of life in Iceland, with taste and respect. And because he had come to Iceland to find out, rather than to defame and exploit, he was able to report also that there was a remarkable discrepancy between their physical circumstances and their civilized manners and intellectual attainments. It appears from Donald Sage's journal that this is what a cultured Englishman visiting Strathnaver in 1810 might have discovered also.

* *The Norseman,* ix, 170.

Indeed, the posthumous publication of Sage's memoirs ought to have dissipated any remaining doubts of this. 'There is no independent middle class to speak out,' an English Member of Parliament had wisely observed in 1845: and Stewart of Garth had foretold in 1822 the social consequences of sweeping away the native lease-holders. But an offspring of the manse and the *tigh mór*, the bighouse in which the junior branches of the chief's family had once lived in Melness and Skerray, Kirtomy and Strathy, one of these, if only a solitary one, had left an unimpeachable record. And to reinforce Sage's record children of the crofters themselves had appeared before the Napier Commission, John Mackay the civil engineer from Hereford, Angus Mackay the clan historian, Hew Morrison the editor, and Ewen Robertson the bard. As to whether Sellar and Loch and the Countess-Duchess had been torch-bearers of civilization in the dark places which reared such men, it might appear that the last word had been said.

But it is of the essence of this tragic story that the last word had not been said. It remained for a Gaelic speaker who had lived half a century on the Sutherland estates to demonstrate that a people can hardly be brought to the brink of destruction without some rottenness at the core: in Evander MacIver's memoirs this rottenness is left festering. MacIver is indeed little more than a buffoon, but his countrymen in north Scotland were in a predicament that could ill withstand his form of foolery.

Loch had commended those few native middlemen who had co-operated in his ventures, 'seconding the views of the landlords with the utmost zeal, marked with much foresight and prudence'. But the nature of their co-operation might have remained somewhat obscure and their motives beyond the skill of divination, but for the revelations of Evander MacIver.

He was born at Gress in the island of Lewis in 1811, just after the first evictions had taken place in Sutherland. 'The Gress family', he noted, 'were always considered respectable and superior, and they connected with superior families on the mainland.' Rob Donn had been a guest of his forebears at Gress, and had celebrated their hospitality in the graphic poem which tells of the hazards of the sea-journey, and of the excited cluster of women heard whispering on their arrival: '*O chiall,*

am bheil e posd?'—Gracious, do you think he's married?
Evander's great-grandfather on his mother's side was Rob
Donn's contemporary James Robertson, the formidable minister
remembered as *Am Ministeir Laidir*, whom Evander commemorated with pride. He himself entertained John Campbell
of Islay, one of Europe's outstanding folklorists, who published
the Fingalian ballads and the West Highland Tales. He helped
also to obtain a civil list pension for the collector of the *Carmina
Gadelica*, and he was acquainted with Dr. Norman Macleod,
whose book *Caraid nan Gaidheal* is one of the monuments of
modern Gaelic prose. So when Evander described his family as
'superior', it might be thought that he used the term in a Celtic
context and in a cultural sense. But this was not in the least
what he meant.

His grandfather had died in debt, but his father had made
himself the richest man in Stornoway by successful speculation
in cattle, fish-curing, and ship-owning. 'He had received a very
imperfect education,' recorded his son, 'and he gave me a first-
class training, first in Stornoway, and latterly for five years in
Edinburgh.'

What Evander considered to be an imperfect education in a
Highlander can only be inferred from his memoirs. His sole
reference to education in Stornoway is that 'the better classes in
Stornoway were not satisfied with the parish school, attended
as it was by children from whom infectious complaints were
caught, and many of whom could not speak English.' He was
early protected against such infections as measles and Gaelic,
for 'the parents of the upper classes in Stornoway united and
became bound to pay a yearly salary to a good teacher, and they
had the use of a large room in the Masonic Lodge of the town as
a school. . . . I was among the youngest, and was taught only
English and a little arithmetic.'

Evander reached Edinburgh in 1825. The general attitude to
a Hebridean in the city and the year in which Stewart of Garth
published the third edition of his book is hinted at suggestively
in MacIver's memoirs. 'I was laughed at for my Stornoway
intonation and pronunciation, and soon got rid of part of it; but
when excited or in a hurry it broke out unknown to me for
months after my arrival, which was really painful to me on
several occasions.' He referred, of course, to his intonation of

English. The capital and university city of Scotland, which had continued to purvey James Macpherson's English prose Poems of Ossian as the authentic translations from a third-century Scottish Gaelic epic long after the fraud had been exposed in Ireland and England, would have greeted MacIver with louder laughter if he had used his native tongue.

Perhaps it was at this time that Evander learned to defend himself with the assertion that he belonged to a 'superior' family despite his Gaelic accent. Since he wrote his memoirs (as it appears) towards the end of his long life, it is impossible to pronounce with certainty on the part Edinburgh played in turning Evander into a lickspittle and a snob. But before he had passed from school to university there, as he was able to reassure himself later, 'I had now acquired the manners, ideas, and appearance of an Edinburgh-bred boy'. While this must not be allowed to reflect on all the other Edinburgh-bred children who were his contemporaries, it is perfectly clear what Evander understood by such manners and ideas.

From the university he progressed through the offices of various factors in the Lowlands and the Highlands, until in 1845 he was appointed by James Loch a factor on the Sutherland estate. This appointment must rank as one of the most perspicacious of Loch's career.

MacIver was given for his home the Duke's house at Scourie on the west coast, from where he could see his native island of Lewis on a clear day. Here he found himself instantly involved in the operation of the new Poor Law of 1845. 'It gave me much to do and think of, organizing and setting it agoing, added much to my travelling, attending meetings in the several parishes, restraining the number of applications, and fixing the allowances.' Even though the Duke's factor possessed this dictatorial power over the amount of relief and over the very right to it, MacIver showed only grudging approval for a measure which, 'though a blessing and comfort to many poor creatures, has proved a very severe tax on the landlords and tenants and people of Scotland'.

There was worse to come. 'This was followed in 1846 and following years by the potato disease, a terrible visitation, over the north and west of Scotland in particular, for the small tenants and crofters lived principally on potatoes and fish; these poor and small crofters grew few oats. Bere and barley was the grain almost universally produced on their small lots or patches of arable land. It created a panic in the minds of landlords and their agents, and the small tenants were almost overwhelmed with terror as to their future support.'

The next passage in MacIver's memoirs is profoundly interesting. 'The Sutherland family had been kind to their small tenants. The feeling created by the introduction of sheep in the early years of the century, and by the clearances in Strathnaver, which were carried out in a harsh and ruthless manner by some of the parties who acted for the Sutherland estate, and by removals of crofters to make way for sheep, had generated a strong rebellious tendency in the minds of the lower classes in Sutherland against their superiors . . . An innate sense of wrong and injury by landlords, agents and sheep farmers towards small tenants appeared to fill the minds of many.' Thus MacIver defended his employers against the reputation he attributed to the actions of Sellar and his accomplices. Not even MacIver would defend Sellar himself.

He confirmed, incidentally, the charge of Donald Macleod that famine relief was barred from the Sutherland estate. 'When the potato disease broke out in the years 1846–47–48, committees of relief were formed over England and Scotland, and much money was subscribed for the benefit of the small tenants and cottars. . . . The Duke of Sutherland gave intimation to these committees that he was not to accept of any of their funds, that he would himself undertake to provide food and employment on his estates.'

Evander MacIver was never in doubt as to the proper solution to the appalling conditions that faced him when he was appointed factor at Scourie. The Celtic people should emigrate *en masse*, leaving their country to the large stock tenants and the sporting landlords who visited the steadily increasing wilderness for their recreation. 'Since 1872 education has become more general. Formerly the Gaelic language was their sole language, and this prevented them from migrating southwards for employment. English is now commonly spoken, and the young people leave home and go south for employment in the towns as servants in private houses, assistants in shops, and into stores and hotels.' Evander himself was tireless in promoting this object.

On one occasion he took the matter up with the Duke's factor: 'I recommended Mr. James Loch, the commissioner on the estate, to take up the question seriously. He at once cordially entered into my views, and the consequence was that in the three following years nearly a thousand people emigrated, principally to Upper Canada and Cape Breton: an immense blessing for most of those who went, and a valuable relief in the various parishes of this district.' Evander was perhaps spared the knowledge that these people had obstinately carried their native language with them, or that one of the most blistering poems about their treatment in Sutherland was published in Prince Edward Island before his own memoirs.[21]

In Evander's view the world was so large that there was no excuse for anyone to remain at home. 'I was asked by the municipal authorities of Shanghai in China to select and send out to them some stout and healthy young men to act as policemen. I sent a considerable number; but they did not like the climate, and most of them emigrated to Australia.' They escaped Evander's censure only because they did not attempt to return home. He wrote sharply to a relative in Texas who proposed to come back to his native country. Of his relative Dr. Roderick Ross, who did not leave Lewis at all, he commented: 'He is a very intelligent well-read man, and highly esteemed as a medical man and as a scholar in his native country, where he has spent his life in the practice of his profession—lost, in my opinion, in a poor remote country district, containing seven thousand people, almost all poor crofters, where he receives a limited income from the parish and next to nothing from his numerous patients.'

But Evander did not himself emigrate, as he encouraged so many of his fellow countrymen to do. He remained in the factor's house at Scourie from 1845 until his death nearly sixty years later; and there, in his retirement, he wrote the reminiscences that were published after his death as the *Memoirs of a Highland Gentleman*. 'There is no duty I performed during my services as factor in Sutherland,' he was able to reflect at the close of his long life, 'on which I look back with more satisfaction than the time, trouble, and care I expended in carrying out the transportation of so many families from the poor position of crofters in a wet climate and a poor soil for cultivation, to the more fertile lands of Canada, Nova Scotia, and Australia. The crofter system has not within it the seeds of prosperity or of profit.'

He could not mean, of course, that the country as a whole was unprofitable. 'William Gunn came to Sutherland in 1832 with £500,' he noted elsewhere, 'and he left £25,000 to be divided among his heirs.' All he could mean was that the native people had no access to the source of such profits, and that the little they did hold they could not improve because they did not possess the security of ownership.

Other Highlanders, Lowlanders, and Englishmen were concerning themselves with this anomaly as a matter of urgency, seeing how fast Gaelic society was being destroyed before their very eyes. Of such men Evander wrote with extreme severity. 'A vast deal of ill-feeling was exhibited all over that part of Skye,' he observed of the case Professor Blackie had also reported, 'and by degrees it spread all over the north, and cases of hardship, of removal, of oppression, and cruelty were published and spoken of. Crofters as a rule held their crofts as yearly tenants, and there were few or no estates on which, in the necessary discipline of management, cases of removal could not be cited and described in violent language. Agitators for their own aggrandisment and selfish purposes sprang up here and there, and latterly everywhere.'

It had been easier, in earlier days, to attach such labels to Donald Macleod than MacIver now found it to apply them to Gladstone. The great Liberal statesman visited Lochinver as the guest of the Liberal third Duke, and the Duchess 'introduced me as a Highlander who was full of Highland information. I thus had long talks with Mr. Gladstone, and spent a most delightful week in his company.' A man so little like an agitator of selfish purposes could only, in Evander's opinion, be wanting in judgement. 'The impression I formed of Mr. Gladstone was that he was too impetuous in coming to conclusions, too easily impressed by what he heard'—though not, it seems, during that week in Lochinver—'and he did not appear to me to be a man of that strong judgment and common sense necessary for those who are to be guides of men or parties.' It was Evander's method of illuminating the truth to praise those who shared his own opinions, and to attack the characters of those whose views differed from his own. He did the same with Gladstone as a matter of course.

At Scourie, Evander MacIver observed the gradual consummation of Gladstonian error and unscrupulous agitation. 'The agitation of crofters, and the Report of the Commission appointed to inquire into the complaints of the crofters, culminated in the passing of the Crofters Act, which introduced a principle as law into Scotland, which I believe does not exist in any other part of the world, viz. that an owner in possession of land in certain Highland counties cannot manage his own estate when the lands let are under thirty pounds of rent; and that an occupant of such land, called a croft, can complain as to his rent and other matters to three Crofter Commissioners appointed by this Crofter Act to decide between landlord and tenant.

'Thus has been created a dual ownership, which actually deprived landlords, without any compensation, of the management of their own estates occupied by crofters, gave the crofters security of tenure if they paid their rents and observed the conditions of this Act. A landlord who has a crofter as tenant cannot now remove him, although he be convicted of dishonesty, theft, or immorality of the grossest description, or be unjust to his neighbours, or have the most disreputable character among them.' MacIver wrote this in the twentieth century. He believed that his Celtic countrymen should be disciplined, not by the laws of the land, but by a private code such as the Loch laws, imposed by a landlord who might be an American or an Indian maharaja.

He made no secret of the clause in the old code that he valued most. The loss of the landlord's power to evict 'has had the effect of stopping emigration to a better climate and soil, where the industrious steady labourer is sure to live in comfort, and become the proprieter of the land he may improve'. The Gaels might own and improve land in other parts of the world, but not in their own country. The Highlands and islands were fit for proprietors to live in, but unfit for their indigenous inhabitants. Here in Evander's memoirs is the opposite thesis to the one expressed by Malcolm MacCallum in the Commission's Report of 1892: 'The solution of the Highland problem is not land purchase, but the resumption of the clansmen's right to occupy the Fatherland.'

Of the society which instead owned the fatherland, and which visited it during the summer season, Evander has preserved many fascinating glimpses. He became in the end the servant of two English dukes, of Sutherland and Westminster, and the respect and gratitude they extended to him is marked by his occupation of Scourie House until his death, so that he was able to call himself MacIver of Scourie, as though he himself were a landed proprietor. Sharing the views of the proprietors and the language and blood of the inhabitants, he was in a unique position to earn such respect and such emoluments.

How tenderly Evander's susceptibilities were nursed he himself described. 'I was treated kindly, courteously and generously by the Duke of Westminster, corresponded with himself direct.' Incremental repetition in a wide variety of contexts throughout the memoirs clarifies the relationship. 'Members of his family known to me as children, but now with families of their own, talk of having been visitors at Scourie House in their childhood, and thus treat me as a very old friend.'

His relationship with the Sutherlands had begun in 1845, not with an interview with the second Duke in Scotland, but with breakfast with his wife in London. 'I was asked to accompany Mr. James Loch, commissioner on the Sutherland estate and Member for the Northern Burghs, to breakfast at Stafford House; and on our arrival there I was shown into the breakfast-room, and Mr. Loch left me.' The kilted retainers who had been paraded for Harriet Beecher Stowe do not seem to have been required to welcome the Hebridean. 'I found a young red-haired man reading a newspaper, who very affably asked me to excuse his reading a most interesting debate he had listened to the previous night in the House of Commons. This turned out to be the young Duke of Argyll, who had married the previous year the eldest daughter of the Duke of Sutherland. The Duchess presided at breakfast. The Duke was not present. They were all most pleasant.'

As the two English dukes perambulated their guests round their Highland estates, Evander's noble and royal acquaintance grew in the most gratifying manner. 'In 1873 the Princess Christian was at Lochmore, and Lady Constance drove her down to Scourie, and called for Mrs. MacIver, on which occasion I was not at home. Mrs. MacIver did not expect the visit, but fortunately she was able to provide what was necessary in a mishap which befell, for which the Princess expressed her warmest thanks, kissing Mrs. MacIver when leaving.'

Others were less careful to observe the form of treating the Duke's servant as his friend, and the laird of Scourie recorded such facts with surprising candour. Sir William Harcourt once ordered Evander to send a horse to Ullapool with a telegram, and was described as speaking 'in a style indicating that he was superior to all present'. The other people present were perhaps less sensitive to this than Evander. When he described John Bright as 'the most uncouth ill-tempered man I had ever met in his rank!' he was possibly referring to Bright's politics rather than his personal treatment of the superior Highlander.

But his most copious memories were of the kiss his wife got from a Princess, his personal friendship with dukes, his intimacy with the great. It was a most fitting tribute when his memoirs were published after his death through a subscription headed by the Dukes of Teck, Sutherland, and Westminster. There were no Mackays among the subscribers and scarcely any natives of the country in which he had spent nearly sixty years: but if he had had his way there would have been none of these left to subscribe.

His editor remarked that Loch's *Account* was 'a work to him of special interest'. He also wrote of MacIver that 'he had the spirit and capacity of the best of the dictators of olden times, and had he not lived his life in so remote a corner, he would have easily ended in the peerage'. But MacIver himself called Scourie a perfect bottle-neck of migrant royalty and nobility, and wondered whether he could ever have made acquaintance with so many in any other place or capacity. And this appears to have been his sole and sufficient justification for flouting the advice he pressed upon others, by remaining in his native land. He could not even resist committing to paper his delight in fawning on the foreign masters who were yet more superior than himself, and in showing their guests the romantic splendours of his devastated country.

For a devastation it was, and remains to this day for all to see, a ruined land almost entirely owned by absentee proprietors who require a wilderness for their holiday recreations.

How such an enormity could ever have occurred, here in this

cradle of democracy, in times so close to our own, is a matter for most worthwhile study. It is apparent that greed played a part, as it does in most human affairs. In a sufficiently well-ordered society untrammelled greed will often lead a man to the criminal courts: at other times in history it has set men on imperial thrones or enabled them to dominate the financial affairs of nations. Absentee landownership offers a particularly strong temptation to the predatory, as the history of Latin America and the British Isles especially reveals: and Mexico can instance its Sellars, Lochs, and MacIvers even later in time than Scotland. In both countries it was the unrestricted underling on the make who proved to be the most poisonous product of the system, sometimes no less to the landlord than to his peasants.

His depredations may have been perfectly legal where the laws of the land were sufficiently iniquitous, as Sismondi noticed, and they may even have been justified by appeals to public as well as private interest. Often such arguments belong to the theories and the climate of opinion of the day, and Loch cannot be accused of deceit because he took his pick of the economic theories that were being expounded by such men as Professor Nassau Senior. Even in a man so naturally deceitful there is likely to have been a margin of sincerity.

There also appears in his attitude to the Highlands an element that was no private weakness of his own: it has been general among the English-speaking Lowlanders from the time of their first settlement north of the Border to the present day. Loch, like Sellar, was undoubtedly actuated by the strong racial prejudice about which Stewart of Garth warned his readers.

It is a hidden strand through the whole of British history, this antipathy of the English-speaking peoples for the surviving speakers of the Celtic languages in our islands. In the case of Catholic Ireland it was long based on fear, and later fanned by religious intolerance: and these two have perhaps occasioned more cruelty even than greed between man and man. It reached its horrible climax in Ireland in the potato famine, and it is hard to believe that so many people would have been allowed to suffer so terribly if they had not been considered (perhaps only subconsciously) as not quite human, with their unintelligible language and alien religion.

Lowland Scots possessed their own reasons for sharing the same prejudice, although after the failure of the Forty-Five religion played a far smaller part. On the other hand they were influenced by a circumstance that did not obtain among the English-speakers south of the Border. The very name Scot which they used belongs originally to the Gaels, and so does the national dress which Lowlanders were already adopting with enthusiasm in Loch's day. Yet throughout Scottish history the Gaels had maintained their separate identity and language, as Stewart of Garth pointed out, scorning 'the authority of a distant Government which could neither enforce obedience nor afford protection'. The resentment of the Lowlanders would perhaps have burned less destructively if they had been loved and revered as fellow Scots by the Gaels.

The integration of the reluctant Gaelic Scots with the Lowlanders claiming kinship was virtually completed by the nineteenth-century evictions. 'That barrier which the prevalence of the Celtic tongue presents', as Loch described it, has been destroyed almost throughout the mainland of Scotland, while Edinburgh scholars continue in the task of creating a 'Scots' national language out of the Lowland dialects of English. Sellar, Loch, and the Countess-Duchess appear at this distance in time ás the end-products of a long historical process, whatever their private motives may have been.

So, alas, does the Chief of Mackay who sold the last independent territories of his clan in Strathnaver to the house of Sutherland in 1829. He must have known of Sellar's acquittal in 1816 and Loch's *Account* published in 1820. He could not have been ignorant of what occurred in Strathnaver during 1819–20, and he conducted his acrimonious correspondence with Sellar during the same period. If he shared the views of Stewart or Bakewell or Sismondi, the Chief of Mackay did not show it when he sold the lands his clansmen had occupied before ever their Chief received the first charter of ownership under Edinburgh's laws. Various explanations for his conduct have been offered. It has been suggested that the house of Sutherland deliberately involved him in debt, and then foreclosed on their security. It has been pointed out that his only child was an illegitimate daughter, while the heir to the peerage of Reay was a brother whom he did not wish to succeed to his property also. Nobody succeeded to it, for the greater part of the price paid for it was lost in an unlucky speculation.

But whatever the circumstances, there is no fitter comment on Lord Reay's action than that published by Sismondi eight years after the event. 'Before reaching such a barbarous resolution it had been necessary for the nobleman to cease utterly to share the views, attachment and sense of decency of his fellow men. It had been necessary not merely for him to believe himself no longer their father or their brother, but even to have ceased to believe himself of the same race. It had been necessary for an ignoble greed to extinguish in him the sense of consanguity to which their ancestors had trusted when they had bequeathed the destiny of their people to his good faith.'

Such was the pattern of Highland chiefs that James VI had dreamed of creating, and during the two intervening centuries his policy had prospered deplorably. The record of the Macdonald chiefs and landowners at the time of the evictions is particularly shameful, so that the humanity of the Macleods of Dunvegan in their midst, who impoverished themselves in their attempt to feed starving islanders, stands out in high relief. But not one of these chiefs, with all their pride of race, education and social influence, did as much to bring the plight of their people before the conscience of civilized Europe as the Englishman in Staffordshire, the Member for Rochdale, or the Swiss scholar. There was no effective response from the chiefs to General Stewart's plea, and the Gaelic poetry composed after his time reflects the growing disillusion of his race. It is a minor wonder of our own day that any respect is still paid to the concept of clan chiefship; even in its surviving milieu, the social gathering in Edinburgh or the association of heirs to a clan name in Australia, New Zealand, and America.

There is little trace of such respect among the remaining population of Strathnaver, still protected by statute in the few acres their fathers occupied as tenants at will sixty years ago. What survives is mutual loyalty, reinforced by the strange circumstance that this is perhaps the last part of Britain in which many people still possess four grandparents all having the same name. It is still *Duthaich 'Ic Aoidh*, the land of the Mackays.

Their communities are confined almost entirely to the north

and the west coasts, where they enjoy security of tenure solely for agricultural purposes and cannot dispose of the house they built nor even use it as a boarding-house for tourists without a landlord's permission. There is some lobster fishing at Skerray, over forty miles from the nearest railway station, and Kirtomy has reared one skipper of prodigious catches who operates from Scrabster in Caithness. His more elderly neighbours witnessed from the cliffs the Kirtomy drowning in the days when the young men there still attempted to use their treacherous *geo* as a port. Ewen Robertson once remarked that the only safe haven between Loch Eriboll and Caithness was the port of eternity, and few of the coastal dwellers any longer try to gain a sea-living as they were forced to do in the days of the *Heather-Boat*. It is the atomic station at Dounreay in Caithness which offers the firm foundation of employment for all; for all, that is, who live within its reach by daily bus along the north coast road. West of Tongue the native communities are dying, even in the coastal villages, while the fishing and game resources rise to ever higher values among the successive owners of the lodges.

Inland, except for such rare areas of resettlement as the lower Naver valley, it is a no-man's-land over which the sporting visitors roam in the summer time.

> Mile on mile on mile of desolation,
> League on league on league without an end.

So Swinburne described his journey through it. In ever-extending districts of these vast hinterlands the Forestry Commission is now active, fencing, ploughing, and building the roads for new plantations. Soon the ruins of Rossal, where Chisholm lived and Donald Macleod was reared and the Rev. Donald Sage listened to the long-silenced ballads of Ossian, soon these scenes of heartbreak will be ringed with trees. Life will never return to them and they will be hidden from the windows of Patrick Sellar's house at Syre.

Notes

1. The Gordons evidently hoped to acquire a hereditary peerage title to Strathnaver, which they anticipated in the 18th century by inscribing it in stone on their buildings at Dunrobin. But in the absence of Letters Patent from the Crown, the only valid source of such a title, it was never clear whether the term was supposed to represent the little township of that name in the Naver valley, the valley itself, or the original province which extended from Cape Wrath to the Caithness border. When the Sutherland Peerage case came before the House of Lords in 1771, the bogus title was never mentioned by any party to the dispute. The winning claimant, Elizabeth, Countess of Sutherland, married the Marquess of Stafford, and by 1833 this pair enjoyed every hereditary title from Duke to Baronet by legitimate grant. By then they had also purchased the whole of Strathnaver: but such ownership does not of itself create a peerage title.

2. Immediately after Sellar's acquittal, Lady Stafford's Commissioner James Loch wrote to her that he 'was really guilty of many very oppressive and cruel acts.'

3. This was the year in which they dispensed with the services of Sellar, though Dr Philip Gaskell stated in *Morvern Transformed* in 1968 that he 'continued to clear farms in Sutherland for his employers until 1819 and then retired from their service to devote himself to sheep-farming at [*sic*] Strathnaver.' In fact he was clearing them for himself, watched anxiously by the Countess, who showed herself to be aware of how her reputation had suffered at his hands. In 1817 she wrote a warning letter to Loch: 'we must not give him any promise of entry unless sure of being able to keep it.' She added, 'Sellar is too sly and refining upon his plans by concealing half.' That same October Loch told a colleague, 'I regret

155

as much as you do that Sellar was continued as he has been.' He admitted it was his fault. 'I have however told everybody that it is only a temporary measure.'

4. It was the 7th Lord Reay who sold his entire estates of western Strathnaver to the Staffords in 1829. In 1889 Lord Napier commented in a letter to John Mackay, known as Hereford, who had been a delegate at the Crofter Commission hearings, saying that the Reay family 'had no conscience, and as it turned out no means of fulfilling their engagements.' This line of the chiefs became extinct in 1875, when the title passed to descendants of the 2nd Lord Reay who were already ennobled in the Netherlands. Excerpts from Napier's previously unpublished letter appeared in *Sar Ghaidheal: Essays in Memory of Rory Mackay*, a descendant of Hereford.

5. Napier was as satisfied as the General had been that arson of dwelling houses had occurred, having likewise questioned witnesses personally. He told Hereford in his letter of 1889: 'I never had any doubt either of the burning of the cottages or the violation of the promises . . . The burning of the dwellings was the natural, almost inevitable result of the cruel policy of eviction.' In 1959 the Revd R. I. Mackay stated the same as a descendant of William Mackay, one of the delegates who had given evidence before Lord Napier in what is now the Strathnaver Museum. William had been 'a measg na muinntir a bha air am fuadachd bho Srath Nabhair. 'S iomadh uair a chuala e mar a chaidh na dachaighean sin a bhriseadh gu làr, an àirneis a thilgeadh a mach 's an taighean air a chur na theine.' Professor Rosalind Mitchison has dismissed all such memories with the assurance: 'on Sutherland the verbal tradition of the crofters, as presented to the Napier Commission, is peculiarly unreliable.' She offered no grounds for this delphic pronouncement, which appeared in *Scottish Economic and Social History* (1981). She did, however, commit herself to the verdict: 'The picture of Sellar resorting to force is unproved and at odds with what we know of his character.' This is directly at variance with the judgements of Lady Stafford and James Loch, to whom Sellar was known personally.

6. In 1799 Lady Stafford learned that her kinsman General Wemyss contemplated withdrawing from his recruitment campaign in Sutherland because of the poor response. She wrote to her factor John Fraser: 'I would have him do it, or at least threaten to do it if they do not come in in a certain time, as they are really unworthy of his attention, and need no longer be considered as a credit to Sutherland or any advantage *over sheep* or any other useful animal.' A black-list was compiled of those 'tenants of Kildonan who thought

proper in the course of the recruitment to show a preference of other Regiments to those which the Marquis and Marchioness recommended.' Their families were evicted at the next term. Those who joined the 93rd Regiment in total subservience assumed their families would be safe, and it was the breaking of the promises to these that Lord Napier described with particular severity to Hereford, comparing the behaviour of the Reay and Sutherland families. 'In the Sutherland family the faithlessness was the more inexcusable, but their conscience seems to have been perverted by bad counsel and false theories of social management.'

7. Two brothers published religious poetry at this time. One collection was *Dantadh Spioradal*, Clodh-bhuailt airson U. G. le Deorsa Conolie, Leabhar-reiceudair Gaeleadh 1802. This was Uilliam Gordon, described as 'Saighidfhear ann an Reighiseamaid Mhic-Aoi.' His brother George Ross Gordon left the Reay Fensibles in 1802 and served in the 42nd Regiment in Ireland, where he published his poems in about 1804. He died in Creich in 1820.

8. Strathy had been alienated earlier. John of Strathy disponed his estate to his grandson Sir William Honeyman Baronet of Graemsay in Orkney, who sold it to the Marquess of Stafford in 1813 for £25,000.

9. The character of the Countess-Marchioness-Duchess remains controversial. Thomas Creevey remarked from personal acquaintance that she had the appearance of 'a wicked old woman.' The more of her letters that come to light, the more unpleasant she reveals herself to be.

10. The evidence that Donald MacLeod was indeed present, and that he was considered at the time to be credit-worthy, is provided by the fact that Sellar cited him as a witness.

11. The Revd R. I. Mackay alluded to this threat in his description of the parting between Donald MacLeod and his grandfather William Mackay. His home was in Strathy, which had belonged to the Sutherland estate since 1813. 'Mu dheireadh leig Domhnull inntinn suas dol do Chanada, far nach cuireadh maor neo bàillidh eagail air daoine bochda. Chuir e roimhe ᵣ..us falbhadh e gun toireadh e sgrìob dheireanach a fhaicinn tìr-a-dhaoin. Air a thuras, rainig e Strathaidh agus gnog e air dorus Uimmeam 'ic Aoidh. Chuireadh fàilte agus furan air agus dh'iarradh air tighinn a stigh.'

'O cha tig,' fhreagair Domhnull. 'Nach eil fhìos agad, Uilleam, gu de dh'eireas dhuit ma leigeas tu mise thar leac an doruis?'

'Coma leat-sa sin,' fhreagair Uilleam. 'Bha mi air m'fhuadach dà uair mar tha, agus cha thacair nas miosa nan treas uair co dhiùbh. Thig thusa stigh is fheudar duit tighinn cuide ruinn agus fuireach

NOTES

maille ruinn. Bochd is mar a tha sinn, tha cuid na h-aoidh daonnan againn airson caraid.' Such are the folk whose testimony Mitchison has dismissed as 'peculiarly unreliable.'

12. Anderson had obtained his lease from Lord Reay before the estate was sold in 1829, and it did not expire until 1846. Richards has pointed out, in *A History of the Highland Clearances* (1982), 440–4, that both the 2nd Duke and his Commissioner Loch were angered by his actions. The episode was described in a poem by Donald Mackay, composed when he was over eighty years old, first published in 1899 in volume XXIV of the *Transactions of the Gaelic Society of Inverness*.

Bha mise ann an Smò a linnibh nam Fiann,
Nan laoch sin nach teicheadh gun fhuil thoirt á bian;
Cha chuimhne leam batail a chunna' mi riamh,
Gun duine ann nach seasamh ri clobha no liagh.

'N tràth thàinig na Cataich, bu spalpail an ceum,
Is dùil ac' ri creach thoirt an Crasg uainn do leum,
Gun duine 'nam feachd chumadh buille no beum
Ri mnathan Cheann-abin, buaidh thapaidh leo féin.

'Na tràth chunnaic na gaisgich na h-armagan rùisgte
An clobha, 's an corran, an cabar, 's an t-sùist;
Chlisg iad le feagal, is thubhairt cuid dhiù,
'S miosa so do na Cataich no cath Dhruim-na-cùb.

'Feadh bha iad san Dùrin, bha cùisean orr' teann,
Ged thàirr iad dh'an Inn, cha b'fhad' dh'fhan iad ann;
Gun ørachadh bìdh', no dibhe, no dràm,
Chuir pìob Dhomh'll 'ic Cullaich iad uile do dhanns'.

Aig Tobair-a-chrib ann am priobadh na søl,
Bha'n *Countari-dance* a bha annasach ùr;
'S ged chosinn MacCullach le phìobaireachd cliù
'S olc chumadh na fleasgaich ud *step* ri chuid ciùil.

'S bhuail an *retreut* aca le cabaig is caoir,
Ruith Siorra' is Fiscal, Polisich 's Maoir;
Bha cuid ac a' canntainn "bithidh an gnothach dhuinn daor
Mar fhàir sinn ar falach air taobh eile a' chaoil."

Gun fhuil thoirt air neach aca, ghlan theich iad air falbh,
Cuid ris an aonach, is cuid feadh an arbh';
Bùidsear Dhòrnaich gun fheòl thoirt do'n arm
Gu madainn Di-Dòmhnaich san eòrna leith-mharbh.

158

13. *Quarterly Review* (1842), LXIX, 419.
14. An indictment of the Board of Supervision was published in Inverness in 1855 with the title *The State of the Highlands in 1854*.
15. News of Loch's death was greeted by an explosion of public joy in the northern Highlands.
16. Blackie's book is perhaps the first to have merited the accolade of Dr Gaskell's stricture concerning 'popular historians who have been interested chiefly in the propagandist or sentimental aspects of the subject.' Gaskell's *Morvern Transformed*, published in 1968, also scoffed at 'the absurdity of the Sellar folklore which still persists in Scotland' and earned him the epithet 'cool-headed' from Professor Smout. But Dr James Hunter has singled out Gaskell among those economic historians who have spared hardly a thought for the victims of the estate managements that they study with such meticulous care. 'The people upon whom estate management imposed their policies have been almost completely neglected.'
17. The situation has improved since those words were written. At Farr School, where children were punished if they were heard speaking Gaelic in the playground, even after the Second World War, the language is now taught as a subject of the school curriculum.
18. It was published for the first time in the original edition of this book, with variant versions and the names of those who had supplied them. The following text has been edited by Fred Macaulay.

> Mo mhollachd aig na caoraich mhòr'.
> Càit bheil clann nan daoine còir,
> Dhealaich rium nuair bha mi òg,
> Man robh Dùthaich 'ic Aoidh 'na fàsach?

The refrain runs: 'My curses on the Cheviot sheep. Where are the children of the worthy folk, torn from me when I was young, when the Mackay Country was made a desert?' The poem continues by stating that 'it is three score years and three since we left the Mackay Country.' This was the period that had elapsed between the great clearance of 1819–20 and the year before the Napier Commission began its hearings in 1884. Ewen Robertson had been born in 1842, so his poem enshrined a tradition, not his personal experience.

> Tha trì fichead bliadhn' 's a trì
> On a dh'fhàg sinn Dùtchaich Mhic Aoidh,
> Càit bheil gillean glan mo chrìdh
> 'S na nìghneagan cho bhòidheach?

Loch mo chrìdhe, fhuair thu bàs:
Ma fhuair thu ceartas fhuair thu blàths.
Gun caill an Donas an làmh cheàrr
Mur bi e càirdeil còir riut.

Andersonaich bh'air an ceann
On thog an t-seilcheag suas a ceann,
An t-àit as mios', on cha' thu ann,
Cha d'fhair e ceàrd cho mòr riut.

Bhain-Diùc Chataibh, bheil thu 'd shìth?
Càit bheil his go ghùntan sìod'?
Do chaomhainn iad bho'n fhoill 's bho'n fhrìd
Tha 'g itheamh measg nan clàraibh?

Ceud Diùc Chataibh le chuid foill,
'S le chuid càirdeas do na Goill,
Gum b'ann an Iuthern 'n robh a thoill
'S gum b'fheàrr leam Iùdas làmh rium.

Shellair shalaich tha 'san ùir.
Ma fhuair thu'n gràs ris 'n robh do dhùil,
'N teine leis do chur thu'n tùthadh
Tha fuaim aig nis ri t'fheusag.

The text of another of Ewen Robertson's songs may be found in *Gairm* 41, 1962, pp. 29–31, together with some biographical details. A monument has been raised to the bard's memory near to the spot on Tongue where he was found dead in 1895.

19. His printed copy of the Commission hearings contains marginal notes in his hand such as, 'True, I was a witness,' and 'Quite true, I saw the whole scene.' This is another of the delegates whose testimony Mitchison dismisses as 'peculiarly unreliable.'

20. The book runs to over 400 closely printed pages of considerable importance to the social history of the north of Scotland, most of them unrelated to the clearances. Napier remarked to Hereford when it appeared, 'I am rather sorry that the whole MS, without the least alteration or omission, has not been printed. It may be, however, that the work would have been too voluminous and expensive.' It would have seemed inconceivable that anyone could have doubted the *bona fides* of the author, or the accuracy of what he recorded so privately and in such meticulous detail. Professor Mitchison has risen to the challenge, delivering in 1981 the curt anathema: 'the taint of religious hostility is apparent.'

21. This poem by Domhnall Baillidh (Donald Baillie) appears to have been composed soon after the trial of Patrick Sellar in 1816, although it was not published until 1889 in *The Glenbard Collection of Gaelic Poetry*, Prince Edward Island.

It follows the form and air of a song composed by Alasdair Mac Mhaighstir Alasdair (Alexander Macdonald) after the defeat of the rising of 1745, whose refrain *Hé'n clò dubh* is instantly associated with it by the Gaelic listener. Macdonald was ridiculing the *clò dubh*, the black cloth which his people were forced to wear when the Highland dress was proscribed. Baillie was concerned with the *ceàrd dubh*, the black tinker who enslaved our country'. The use of the epithet *ceàrd* clearly refers to Sellar's trial, at which he had discredited Chisholm the chief witness by describing him as a mere tinker. Verse eight elaborates by calling Chisholm Sellar's brother. It addresses Sellar as follows: 'You yourself went with your associates up to the high ground of Rossal, and demolished the house of your brother by fire.' The poem laments that he was not sentenced to long imprisonment on bread and water, elaborates on severer punishments which would be appropriate, and forecasts in verse nine that when he dies he will not receive decent burial but be flung on a dung-heap. The poem also castigates Young, and the man named Roy whom Angus Mackay, Strathy Point, mentioned during the hearings of the Napier Commission.

> Hó 'n ceàrd dubh,
> Hé 'n ceàrd dubh,
> Hó 'n ceàrd dubh
> Dhaor am fearann!

> Chunnaic mise bruadar
> 'S cha b'fhuathach leam fhaicinn fhathast;
> 'S nam faicinn e 'nam dhùsgadh
> Bu shùgradh e dhomh ri 'm latha.

> Teine mór an òrdagh
> Is Ròy 'na theis meadhoin,
> Young bhith ann am prìosan
> 'S an t-iarunn mu chnàimhean Shellair.

> Tha Sellar an Cuil-mhàillidh
> Air fhàgail mar mhadadh-allaidh,
> A' glacadh is a' sàradh
> Gach aon nì a thig 'na charaibh.

Tha shròn mar choltair iaruinn,
No fiacail na muice bioraich;
Tha ceann liath mar ròn air,
Is bòdhan mar asal fhireann.

Tha 'rugaid mar chorr riabhaich,
Is ìomhaigh air nach eil tairis,
Is casan fada liaghach
Mar shiaman de shlataibh mara.

Is truagh nach robh thu 'm prìosan
Ré bhliadhnan air uisg is aran,
Is cearcall cruaidh de dh' iarunn
Mu d' shliasaid gu làidir daingeann.

Nam faighinn-s' air an raon thu,
Is daoine bhith 'ga do cheangal,
Bheirinn le mo dhòrnaibh
Trì òirlich a mach dhe d' sgamhan.

Chaidh thu féin 's do phàirtidh
An àirde gu bràighe Rosail,
Is chuir thu tigh do bhràthar
'Na smàlaibh a suas 'na lasair.

Nuair a thig am bàs ort
Cha chàirear thu anns an talamh,
Ach bidh do charcais thodharail
Mar òtrach air aodann achaidh.

Bha Sellar agus Ròy
Air an treòrachadh leis an deamhan
Nuair dh' òrdaich iad an combaist
'S an t-slabhraidh chur air an fhearann.

Bha 'n Simpsonach 'na chù,
Mar bu dùthchasach do 'n a' mharaich:
Seacaid ghorm á bùth air,
Is triùsair de dh' aodach tana.

'S i pacaid dhubh an ùillidh
A ghiùlain iad chum an fhearainn-s';
Ach chithear fhathast bàitht' iad
Air tràillich an cladach Bhanaibh.

Index